Randall pulled her into his arms. Swept against his excited, powerfully built body, Jada felt every part of herself weakening. The heated way he looked at her, the addictive way he smelled, his sweet ways toward her, and her emotions that grew with every second around him, all made her helpless when his mouth captured hers. Throughout each rapturous second that he kissed her, he eased her down toward the hardwood floor.

Jada couldn't believe she was about to make love to him and Randall was about to make love to her. Tasting him and holding on to his massive shoulders, she felt so sensually alive it was as if she were eighteen again, in his arms, in that moment, right before they were about to make love. But they had not made love, she reminded herself. He had left her and never returned.

TROPICAL
Heat

LOURÉ
BUSSEY

ARABESQUE

★BET
BOOKS™

BET Publications, LLC
http://www.bet.com
http://www.arabesquebooks.com

ARABESQUE BOOKS are published by

BET Publications, LLC
c/o BET BOOKS
One BET Plaza
1900 W Place NE
Washington, DC 20018-1211

All Kensington Titles, Imprints, and Distributed Lines are available at special quantity discounts for bulk purchases for sales promotions, premiums, fund-raising, and educational or institutional use. Special book excerpts or customized printings can also be created to fit specific needs. For details, write or phone the office of the Kensington special sales manager: Kensington Publishing Corp., 850 Third Avenue, New York, NY 10022, attn: Special Sales Department, Phone: 1-800-221-2647.

First Printing: September 2004
10 9 8 7 6 5 4 3 2 1

Printed in the United States of America

To Brandon Christopher,
You are my greatest blessing

Chapter One

July 1984

As she stepped out of the taxi, a lush, rare breeze swept across Jada Gracen's face from the sultry Savannah air that did nothing to soothe the butterflies in her stomach. She gazed up at the white, Victorian house—her new home for her college years—while the driver opened the trunk to remove her luggage. It was like a dream as she stood before Ms. Emma's boardinghouse, miles away from her family in New Jersey. Ms. Emma's place was also where Randall Larimore stayed during the summer. Perhaps that was the true reason for her nervous tension. Gorgeous Randall Larimore would be in a room right down the hall from hers, according to his sister Kelly.

Blotting a tissue over a light sheen of sweat on her forehead, Jada walked to the back of the cab to help the driver with her suitcases. As she tilted her head down toward the trunk, her plump lips curved gently. Her good friend Kelly came to mind.

Jada appreciated Kelly for asking her father to recommend her as a boarder to their family friend Ms. Emma. Her low rent would minimize Jada's expenses while she attended Savannah State University on a four-year scholarship. Ms. Emma had invited Randall to live at her boardinghouse when he entered Savannah State two years earlier.

Now, he had graduated early with a bachelor's degree in business, but Kelly had shared that he remained in Georgia for the summer because of an internship with a real estate development company. Jada thanked God for that. During the summers she spent at her grandmother's town house in Virginia, she had encountered a man who first made her experience what attraction was—what being sensually alive was—what feeling like a woman was. That male was Randall Larimore. The breath caught in her throat each time she envisioned reuniting with him again.

"Honey, I sure have been looking for you." A rich, elderly woman's voice pierced Jada's musings as if the one spoken to were a missed, beloved relative.

Jada switched her attention from the taxicab's trunk to Ms. Emma's porch. A small-framed woman the color of a penny stood clutching her hips. A hint of a smile tipped up the corners of her lips.

"Ms. Emma?" Jada inquired softly.

The woman's smile broadened, accentuating her high cheekbones. "That's me, honey." Swiftly she reached back for the screen door, cracked it, and yelled into the house, "Gregory, come out here and help this young lady and the driver with her things please."

A husky man that Jada guessed to be in his thirties hurried out of the house. Cheerfulness played across his strong features, softening them as he strutted toward her.

"I'll take these," he said, freeing her hands of two heavy bags.

A small smile touched her lips. "Thank you."

"No problem." Gregory rested the baggage on the pebble-lined walkway and resisted ogling his mother's new boarder. But those eyes and that body he found hard to ignore. "So I heard you're going to be staying with us while you're in college?"

"I'm looking forward to it, too."

"Good. Glad to have you with us. This is my mom's place. I come by most of the time, so you'll be seeing me. But I live farther out by the coast. I'm Gregory." He extended his hand.

She clasped an overly moist palm. "I'm Jada."

"You'll like it here," Gregory informed her proudly. "Just like Randall. You'd think he would leave right after his graduation. But just between you and me, I think the man doesn't ever want to leave here. You see, he's addicted to my mama's cooking."

Jada laughed quietly and wondered where Randall was. "The food is that good, huh?"

"Good isn't the word for it. You'll see. You two grew up together, right? I heard that from either him or my mom."

"Well, we didn't exactly grow up together. My grandmother used to live in Lakeside, the same Virginia town where he's from. I used to visit her every summer and met Randall's sister Kelly, and we became good friends. I saw Randall whenever I visited her. Where is he, by the way?"

"At work," Gregory replied with a glimpse at his watch. "But he should be home soon. He gets off early on Fridays. When was the last time you and Randall saw each other?"

"When I was twelve."

"Oh, I see," he remarked with a memory that secretly tickled him. This morning before Randall headed off to work, he had mentioned that his sister's *little* friend was coming to live at the boarding-house today. Obviously her looks had changed dramatically over the years.

From what Gregory saw, nothing appeared *little* on Randall's sister's friend. She was as healthy as he and his buddies described women with shapely, *banging* bodies. She looked so healthy that Gregory knew Randall was in for a big surprise.

Soon Ms. Emma greeted Jada with a hug that lulled the nerves twisting in the pit of her stomach. Afterward, a tour of the two-story, five-bedroom dwelling made Jada feel more welcome. Ms. Emma valued everyone's privacy. Hence, she avoided showing the bedrooms. She escorted Jada into the living room, den, parlor, kitchen, backyard, and one hallway bathroom. The more Jada beheld, the more she realized that Ms. Emma's interior decorating taste looked just as she had imagined at first sight of the outside of the well-kept house.

Wide-plank, hardwood floors and ceiling medallions blended perfectly with the earth-tone color scheme of russet, beige, and brown. Thick, sinkable couches and chairs beckoned one to laze around on them. Intermingled with antiques, crocheted table mats, and ornament dressings, her home begged one to kick off one's shoes and unwind, rather than admire like a showpiece.

Jada fell in love with the homey atmosphere. It reminded her of her home in Brookshire, New Jersey. What's more, sweet biscuits that Ms. Emma had just baked made the home's scent pure bliss. Randall had told Kelly that Ms. Emma's house always smelled like sweet biscuits even when she wasn't cooking. He assumed the aroma had seeped into the walls and furnishings, almost becoming another adornment in the home.

Once Jada settled into her bedroom, she tucked her clothes in the dresser drawers. Thousands of thoughts scrambled through her head with her adjusting to these new surroundings. Most of all, she wondered about Randall. What would they say to each other? Would he be standoffish or friendly? Would he look as fine as he did years ago?

When she heard a person's movement at the doorway behind her, the unknown presence strangely caused fluttering in her belly. Jada turned around and her heart pound violently. Randall took up the space in the doorway and all the air in the room from her.

It was him, but it wasn't him. Randall's face had matured so much. His fuller jawline made it handsomer. He sported a neat mustache with a goatee outlining his mouth and chin. Close-cropped hair with a trace of waviness emphasized his dreamy features. He towered well over six feet now. A dark blue business suit molded to his broad chest as if it were especially designed for him.

"Jada?" he said unsurely and narrowed his eyes as if questioning his sight.

"Yes, it's me, Randall. I look a little different than the last time you saw me."

His lips inching up in an awkward grin, Randall approached her. In what seemed like slow motion to her, his arms sealed her in a hug. Drugged by his hard body pressed against hers, Jada reciprocated the embrace. It stunned her that he held her like this. She squeezed her eyes tight. Savoring the feel of him, she also inhaled the masculine cologne smell that he exuded.

Her heart thumped faster. Jada felt embarrassed, believing Randall could feel it amid their clinging bodies. Then finally Randall loosened his hold of her and reared back, studying her quietly. His sexy brown eyes scattered over Jada's face with such intensity and bewilderment, she felt tempted to ask him what he was thinking.

"You grew up," he announced with strained silence.

"So did you," she pointed out, awestruck at how magnificent he looked as a full-grown man and clad in business attire.

Randall arched his brows. "I mean you *really* grew up." He laughed lightly.

"I know," she agreed with a bashful grin. "Everyone says that. The last time you saw me I was skinny from my head to my toes. I had pimples and those braces. Your brother Hunter used to get on my nerves about my braces. He had no mercy."

"Oh, he teased everybody, my sisters, who both had braces, and everybody else. He was always the troublemaker. Still is." He chuckled.

"But you weren't. You were always nice to me. I . . .

I mean in those moments that I saw you." She recalled how Randall always spoke to her, even if he never had time to hang around when she spent time with Kelly. He always had to run off with his brothers to play basketball. She would tell Kelly how cute he was as soon as he left. Kelly would tell her she needed eyeglasses.

"It's nice that you and Kelly kept in touch," Randall said, rubbing his chin. "We guys rarely do that. My brothers are the only guys I stay in touch with who knew me when I was a kid. But anyway, what are you doing the rest of the day?"

The question excited Jada so much that her heartbeat felt frozen this time. More than anything, she wanted to be around Randall. "I was just going to hang around here and get settled in."

"On a Friday afternoon?"

"I didn't know what else to do."

"But I do. There are lots of things you can do. I'll show you around. Savannah is an awesome place. And we can catch up."

"That sounds like fun."

"Just let me go change into something more casual."

"Should I change, too?"

Randall's gaze floated down the soft yellow sundress that wrapped her hourglass curves deliciously. A mini, it revealed bare, shapely, well-oiled calves and thighs that made him swallow each time he glimpsed at them. "No, you look . . . you look just fine."

Once Randall entered his room, he locked the door. He wanted to walk around in his underwear and get comfy. In spite of the air conditioner cooling the room, he felt hot. Hot in every way that a man could feel hot.

On his first beholding Jada in the doorway, firmness gripped his loins, a feeling he still hadn't shaken off. He hadn't been this turned on by a stranger in all of his twenty years. And Jada did feel like a stranger. In some way, he was seeing her for the first time.

Randall slipped his arms out of his suit jacket, tugged off his tie, and plopped down on the side of his bed. While removing his cuff links, he mentally retraced those few moments with Jada. She appeared sweet, innocent, down-to-earth, and so fine that no man could deny it. God knows she had changed.

Inside the shower, Randall turned on the cold water, but couldn't turn off thinking about Jada. If he had passed her in the street, he wouldn't have known her. The only thing that remotely resembled her was her eyes. Back in the day, he had never noticed how seductively shaped and mink-colored they were. They looked like the eyes of a mysterious woman he had dreamed of during a late-night fantasy when he lay in bed.

But why was he getting all worked up over one of Kelly's friends? All those little girls that traipsed through his parents' house always felt like little sisters. He had expected that mind-set to continue once Kelly told him that Jada was coming to Savannah State University and would be staying at Ms. Emma's. Now, suddenly after his being in Jada's presence again, she didn't make him feel like a big brother. She made him very much aware he was a man.

But what was wrong with him? Wasn't he acting like his buddies? Most of them desired to jump a woman's bones purely because she was fine. Typical male behavior wasn't his style. His mother even took pride in him being the mature one of her five boys, the one who would covet a woman for her soul and not just her body.

She had come to that conclusion when he brought home Carolyn, his ex. The fellows always taunted him about Carolyn being so skinny and not having any figure. Randall saw beyond that. Carolyn became his queen. What they shared in their world, no one else could feel. No one else could understand it. She made him feel like the happiest man in the world. At least in the beginning of their relationship she did.

Strolling around Savannah's countryside with Randall immersed Jada within sensations comparable to magic befalling her. Sweltering temperatures hardly bothered her. Occasionally gazing over at Randall's handsome profile and being the recipient of his hospitality made anything bearable.

"So what made you pick Savannah State?" Randall asked, admiring the way her flesh shimmered from the sunlight. It had the look of caramel with silk oil poured over it.

Keeping in step with him, Jada reflected on his question. Thanks to her outstanding grades, paired with her family's modest income, scores of colleges offered her scholarships. However, because Kelly had said that Randall highly recommended Savannah State's business program, she researched it and visited the campus. It turned out to be ideal for her.

Being near Randall made the school more attractive. She just hadn't counted on him graduating so quickly. Despite that, spending the summer around him thrilled her.

"After my research and visit to Savannah State, it seemed like the college for me," she said and watched him wipe across his handsome features with a hanky and lower the cloth to his chest and arms exposed in a black tank top. Sun-moistened muscles that she glanced at had Jada losing her train of thought and fanning her face with her hand.

Regaining her focus, she added, "I also came here because I love the country. Georgia has to be one of the prettiest places on the earth."

"Yes, this place is awesome," Randall agreed. He tucked his handkerchief in his back pants pocket and resisted his sudden impulse to latch on to her hand. "I liked the program a lot. That's why I came. On top of that, Savannah is a place with a lot of history. They have lots of homes that have been restored. And they give me ideas about the places I plan to build." For what must have been the hundredth time that day, he glanced down at her pretty legs.

"Oh, that's right. Kelly told me you want to build houses and buildings."

"Yes, that's my thing," he admitted with boyish joy playing over his features. "That's why I doubled up on my courses to get out of school early. I want to own and build lots of houses. That's what I love, and if you follow what you love, you have what's going to make you rich. And I mean rich in every way." He gazed over at her, and her eyes met his.

They also lingered with his. A rush of heat

swooping from Jada's neck to the base of her stomach discomfited her so much that she ripped her eyes away. After a tense moment of silence, she longed to lighten things up by resuming their conversation.

"I feel the same way you do," she told him. "I want to own something of my own. In high school, we had this assignment to run a business from beginning to end. We had to create a product, handle the finances, and so forth. I loved it. I knew then I wanted my own business. I was always fascinated with it because my great-uncle owns a barbershop and a pharmacy.

"He always seems happy, and his family always has enough of whatever they need. He always says to get into business doing something you love. I'm in love with books, so I want to own this really nice bookstore that I visualize in my head. But overall, I'm going to have something of my own to take care of myself and my family."

Impressed, Randall couldn't help smiling at her. "You're all right, Miss Jada Gracen. I like the way you think. You're different from other girls."

"I like the way you think, too," Jada confessed, smiling back at him, only looking away when that heated sensation teased her again. This time it spread, making her thighs clench.

Jada and Randall continued their leisurely walk and interesting tête-à-tête. They wound up in Savannah's Historic District. There they enjoyed each other's company among a backdrop of lush green squares, refurbished houses, old churches, monuments, and pristine sidewalks that granted a pleasant balance of shade and sun. Afterward they explored City Market, a popular shopping area.

Randall's purchasing a dozen red roses for Jada surprised her. No guy had ever given her flowers; that is, except for the corsage she received from her prom date. Randall's roses made her feel delicate. They made her feel feminine. They made her feel as if Randall thought she was as special as she thought he was. They also made her think that possibly he felt this strange but wondrous sensation between them like she did.

Later on, they devoured mouthwatering seafood at an outdoor café. The best part of their time together came at dusk. At that point, they wandered to a serene spot in Forsyth Park. Sitting on the grass, surrounded by trees speckled with Spanish moss, they had a view of joggers running along a path, though everyone and everything was a blur given their fascination with each other.

"I had fun with you today," Randall confessed and didn't hide his growing infatuation with her lips. It had taken every ounce of his strength not to kiss her today.

"I had fun, too." Jada noticed him watching her mouth, and the sultry pulsation flowed through her again. "Thank you for the roses." She gazed at them lying on the ground beside her and fought off an urge to show her gratefulness with a hug, touch, or peck on the cheek or lips. "I feel funny letting you buy them for me. I mean . . . Kelly says you're saving to buy houses and fix them up."

"It was my pleasure to buy you the roses. Consider it a little welcome-to-Savannah gift. I wanted to make you smile." He watched her sensuous smile form, piquing his interest as their eyes met, sharing a secret that he sensed they both felt. "You know, I never noticed your eyes before." His voice dipped low with the revelation.

Her heart raced from his words and gaze. "What about my eyes?"

"They're really pretty. They whisper that you're sexy."

Jada debated how to reply to such a compliment. Was she dreaming this? Had Randall actually said something like that to her? She giggled to camouflage her nervousness. Randall did not join in her amusement. Desire emanated from his expression. She sensed it was the same kind of wanting that stirred within her at that moment.

"Thank you, Randall. Your eyes are very sexy, too."

Randall offered her a closed-lip smile, while his eyes still glistened with need. "You know, I don't usually talk like this to my sister's friends, but there is something special about you, Jada. In just this short time together, I feel that."

"I feel the same way."

"So do you have a man?" Randall asked in a husky voice.

"I had a boyfriend in Jersey," she answered, sounding as soft as she felt beneath his gaze. "He broke up with me before graduation."

"And why would he be fool enough to break up with you?"

Jada laughed lightly. She had called Keith a fool a hundred times herself. "He was going into the army and wanted to marry me. Now, that sounded real good. But then he didn't want me to go to college and didn't want me to work. And he wanted lots of kids. And I love kids. Don't get me wrong. I want to have some one day. I have an adorable baby niece I would do anything for." She watched Randall clutch her hand, and his finger play made her tingle.

"But . . . but I'm only eighteen. At this time in my life, I want to go to college, graduate, get a job, build some income and credit, and then start a business. So he told me he doesn't want a woman who doesn't know how to be a woman and let her man be a man. Then he told me good-bye and went about his business. But I don't care. I wouldn't have been happy with him telling me what to be and how to live."

"I don't see you doing that either," Randall professed, easing closer to her, so that their thighs touched. On contact, the welcome thickness that filled his shorts with each second around her felt like it swelled even more, causing his chest to expand with his rapidly increasing excitement. "You have big dreams just like I do," he said, speaking in a tone much calmer than he felt. "I see you right here strutting your stuff across Savannah State's campus. And I'm glad you're staying at Ms. Emma's. I'm going to be looking forward to seeing you every day."

To that, Jada curbed her impulse to jump up and scream out her joy. "Likewise. So what about you? Any special lady in your life? After all, you've been a college man for a while." She played with his fingers.

Loving her stroking, Randall leveled his gaze at her. "I was with a young lady named Carolyn in Virginia. Actually, we were together since my last year of high school. But we broke up in March."

"What happened?"

"We kind of grew apart with the distance between us. Something was different." He entwined his fingers with hers. "We hardly had anything to talk about anymore when we talked on the phone. And when we visited each other, I didn't feel like I used to feel when we were together—like so high that I couldn't bear for our time together to end. It probably had a lot to do with our different directions in life. She didn't like me saving money to buy property. She wanted me to save up to marry her and buy her a big house." He took her other hand, lacing it with his fingers, too, forcing them to face each other. "But I didn't know if she was the one." Again, he became obsessed with her lips. "Now I know she wasn't."

Wondering if his last words alluded to her being significant in his life, Jada quivered with anticipation. She could tell that Randall intended to kiss her.

But she was curious. "You never wanted to marry her?"

"When we were first together I did. Things were so good then. But later on, I started seeing things in her I disliked. The major one was that she wasn't supportive of my dreams. Then one weekend when I went home, we decided it was over. But we talk from time to time. We're still friends." He bent his head toward her face and her fruity body cream had him wondering about its taste and texture on her skin. Red-hot fire surged through his blood. He heard his ragged breathing, before he whispered, "Enough about them. I'd like to get to know you better. And I'd like to start with this."

His irregular breaths feathered against Jada's cheek and his arms slid around her waist, drawing her close to him. This moment had to be a dream, she told herself. But she knew it wasn't as she felt his hard body crushed against hers. Her nipples hardened. Her eyes fluttered closed. And soon she felt something that had no right to feel so good.

Tasting her as if her every pore filled him with addictive nectar, Randall let his soft lips glide over hers in a butterfly motion until his tongue pierced her mouth. Parting her lips wider, she welcomed him into her warm honey. Again, he titillated her with a butterfly kiss. Then his tongue did a back-and-forth dance that simulated the ebb and flow of lovemaking. All the while, his hands roamed over her back.

A throbbing hit between her thighs from the lusciousness of it all. Breathing in his manly cologne, Jada hoped his kiss would last forever. He tasted like the mints they plopped in their mouths after dinner. But he also tasted like nothing she had ever tasted before—his delicious self. Every part of her burned from the passion he wreaked on her. She fumbled along the mountainlike slopes of his arms until she laced her arms around his neck.

She felt his chest heaving with his every moan. Knowing how much she turned him on fed her own desire. Her fingers slid along his shoulders, enjoying the solidness of them and drawing him closer. His body's hardness intermixed with his painfully sexy kiss drugged her. A waterfall laden with raw need rushed down inside her. Aching for him to inflict more on her, she could barely stand it when he let her go.

"I loved that," he groaned huskily, mashing his lips against her ear. "You taste even better than I thought." He cradled her face within his palms.

Jada brushed her mouth against his finger. "I loved the way you kissed me, too, Randall. I dreamed . . ."

"You dreamed what?"

"Nothing. I just loved it."

Kissing and more kissing aroused Jada well beyond darkness. She was expecting a phone call from her mother, so they had no choice in leaving their love nest in the park. As they strolled home, she loved Randall holding her waist; that is, until they reached Ms. Emma's porch. There she decided they had to be discreet. Randall agreed and let her go.

Sauntering inside the house, Jada relished the aroma of sweet biscuits greeting them. She saw Ms. Emma lounging on a chair, watching television. Across the room, two other borders, Mr. Winston and Mr. Harrell, relaxed on the sofa.

"Good evening, young folks." Mr. Winston, a bald, elderly gentleman, addressed them with a nod of his head.

Mr. Harrell threw his hand up at them.

"Hello, everyone," Jada said.

Randall echoed her words and shuffled over to the TV to see what program they were watching.

"You two have a nice time catching up on old times?" Ms. Emma asked.

"We sure did," Jada answered with a glance at Randall.

He returned her look with a silent expression of satisfaction in his eyes.

"Good," Ms. Emma said, observing the twosome mount the staircase. "That's very good."

* * *

The next morning, Jada awakened in a heavenly
daze. It had to be a dream that she had spent such
a blissful day with Randall. It felt like more of a
dream that he had kissed her over and over again
so passionately. Ecstasy unlike any other poured
through her veins from his lips. No man had ever
kissed her the way he had. Today she couldn't wait
to taste his sweet lips again. First, she had business
to take care of.

She had a job interview at a restaurant and
hoped to spend time with Randall after she returned. However, when he offered to drive her
there and wait for her, Jada was delighted. The college had arranged the interview long before she
left New Jersey. That gave her a reason to come to
Georgia for the summer, rather than the fall when
classes commenced.

Once Randall parked his Grand Am in front of
the Belvedere, one of Savannah's swankiest restaurants, he treated her to a long, tongue-winding kiss.

"Good luck," he uttered from his car window,
admiring her hips swaying as she walked away.
Once she disappeared among the glass swinging
doors, Randall opened the newspaper. He flipped
the pages to the real estate section. Twenty minutes later, he saw Jada practically bounce out of the
restaurant.

"I got it!" she shouted, opening the Grand Am's
door to be with him. She scooted onto the velour
seat cushions beaming. "You're looking at the
Belvedere's latest waitress."

"Aw, Jada, that's wonderful. We're going to cele-
brate." He leaned across the seat and kissed her
long and lingeringly.

Jada lost herself in Randall's hungry kiss and the magic of everything happening to her.

They spent the day doing all sorts of fun activities. Riding in a boat, going to a movie, buying records, and browsing bookstore shelves took up most of their time. When hunger pangs caught up with them for the second time that day, they didn't want to dine at a restaurant like they had earlier.

Randall bought a blanket and then purchased food from a prominent Chinese eatery. Then he drove Jada to one of his favorite secluded places in Savannah. Near the coast, the area rendered a breathtaking portrait of the sea. Adoring the scenery, Randall munched General Tso's chicken, brown rice, broccoli, and egg rolls. He also adored watching Jada licking barbecue sauce off her fingers from the ribs she ordered.

"This is good," Jada commented, before placing another morsel of the tangy meat in her mouth. "Yummy."

Randall became tickled at the way she wolfed down the food. "You're a greedy woman."

"No, I'm not," Jada countered with a playful edge in her voice. "I just don't mess around with food."

"I see that. I guess I'm going to feed you like this all the time."

What he said touched Jada. It assured her that he wanted to spend more time with her. "Randall, I have a confession."

"And what is that?" He bit into an egg roll.

"I used to like you when I was little. I thought you were the cutest thing I had ever seen."

He blushed. "No, you didn't. You're kidding me."

"If you don't believe me, ask Kelly."

"Wow, I had no clue," he said with light laughter.

"I know you didn't. And yesterday, when you kissed me and I was about to say something about dreaming, I was going to tell you that I dreamed about kissing you. I always used to dream about kissing you."

He laid his hand on his chest. "You're making my heart pound like crazy, you know that? What are you trying to do to me?"

She stared at him, feeling her own heart racing. "Let you know what I've been feeling for you. And I really didn't know you before, but in some way I did. I sensed you were nice. And in these last two days, you have been so nice to me."

"I sensed you were very sweet, too," he said. "When I saw you standing in your room, I sensed that. I mean, I knew you a little when we were kids, but I didn't really take the time to get to know you. But when I saw you, I just sensed you were sweet and innocent. And now I feel like I've known you much, much longer. How can that be?"

"I know just how you feel."

He stroked her cheek. "I love kissing you, but I also love talking to you. You seem to understand me, because you're like me. We want to be in control of our lives. We want to own things, and we know it takes hard work to get that. I learned that from my dad. The way he and his partner worked so hard to build their business is really inspiring to me. When they started out, so many people told them that two brothers opening a gourmet dessert company wouldn't work. They said they would be shut out of contracts because of their race. Well, there have been some struggles, but it's working—working real good. My dad is *the man.*"

"I'm happy that you have a good father, Randall."

He talked more about his love, respect, and admiration for his father and mother. He also noticed how Jada glowed when she was speaking about her mother. When he asked about her father, she lowered her head.

Seeing her mood shift, Randall lifted her chin with his fingertips. "What's the matter?"

"I just wish I could say that I learned things from my dad. But he walked out on us when I was nine. When one of my mother's good friends moved away to Chicago to start a new job, he moved with her. My mother was devastated that they had betrayed her that way. I've only seen him once since then. He came to my fourteenth birthday party."

"I'm so sorry to hear that, Jada."

"I'm sorry, too. When he got me alone during the party, he started telling me that my mom always nagged him, and that's why he left her. He said the other woman just wanted to make him happy all the time and she was fun. I sat there and listened, but I wanted to scream at him. I wanted to make him disappear. I wished so bad that he wasn't my father. If my mom had nagged him, it was only because he didn't stand up and uphold his responsibilities. She was the breadwinner in our house. It was her sweat that clothed, fed, and educated me. And I love her more than anything on this earth for it. *I love her.*

"He never did anything for me, except give me heartache. I wished he would go away and never come back." She smiled sadly. "And you know what? My wish came true."

"And you still feel that way about him?"

Jada shrugged her shoulders. "I don't know. I don't know why he couldn't love her. My mother is a good woman. And I don't know why he can't love me. I'm not a bad daughter."

"Jada, don't think that. I'm sure he loves you. Who wouldn't love a daughter as wonderful as you are? The man just doesn't have his act together. Any man that dumps the financial responsibility of taking care of his child all on a woman isn't a real man. He's so lacking and empty inside, he's not worth thinking about.

"And I don't wish anything bad on your dad, but you don't get blessed for things like that. You don't have good luck. Now, your mom, her blessings have been bought and paid for. And if she doesn't have them already, they are on the way. Watch and see."

"That makes me feel good. I hope that's how things turn out."

"That's what my grandparents used to tell us over at the crazy Larimore house. They used to have all seven of us kids sit around them and they would tell us a story. Afterward they would ask us the moral lesson of the story. One theme always came about over and over. And that was that whatever you do comes back to you. If you do good things in the world, good things will come back to you in abundance. If you do bad things, you will receive them abundantly, too. And I don't wish anything bad on your dad, but I know that somehow, and in some way, I bet he's had to pay for something that amounted to the money he never gave your mom and the time he failed to give you."

She looked at him gently. "Your grandparents made a lot of sense. My grandmother says things similar to that."

He leaned closer to her. "And I'll tell you something else. And this is from me. Whatever your dad denies you, it's all because something is wrong within him. Don't ever think you're not worth loving. In these two days I have known you, you have become such an important person to me."

That evening when they returned home, Ms. Emma sat in the living room with Mr. Harrell, watching television again. Immediately she noticed the joy on Randall's face and the sparkle in Jada's eyes.

"My, my, you two have gone out two days in a row. Still catching up?"

"Yes, we are," Randall replied, eyeing Jada. "We're getting to know each other very well."

"So you had a nice time?" Ms. Emma pressed.

Jada lit up. "We had lots of fun. We did some of everything."

"In fact," Randall chimed in, "it was probably the best time I had since I've been in Savannah."

"Really?" Ms. Emma remarked with her gray-brown eyes widening. "The *best* time?"

"The *best*," he responded with a big, contented sigh that raised his chest.

With that, Jada and Randall headed upstairs to their respective rooms as they had the previous night. Ms. Emma watched them both ascending the staircase and pondered what that *best* time consisted of.

* * *

Those moments spent with Randall that day
made Jada feel close and connected to him. She
had shared something with him that she rarely
shared with anyone. She had opened up about something that always felt like a burden on her heart.
The way Randall reacted affected her deeply. His
sentiments brightened that hopeless place inside
her, which she always felt when thinking of her father. Having Randall in her life made her feel that
she was never alone. Even when he wasn't around,
he was with her.

The coming days felt as if they were sprinkled
with stardust to Jada. She became friends with her
coworkers at the restaurant and found most of the
patrons likable. The highlight of each day was
Randall picking her up after work.

They would spend the remainder of the day together. Each second was packed with fun, romance,
and sometimes adventure. Randall introduced her
to golf, tennis, and soccer. Greatest of all, the more
she came to know him, the more she loved about
him. His one negative quality turned out to be jealousy. Jada saw the green-eyed monster in full view
one afternoon.

Randall waited for her shift to end. He chose to
sit at a vacant table in the restaurant instead of his
car where he normally waited for Jada. Reading
the real estate section of the paper, he glanced up
and noticed a blond, forty-something guy holding
on to Jada's hand. She tried to lay the man's check
on the table. Clearly, Jada looked annoyed and
Randall fumed at the sight. He strode over to the
difficult customer.

"Will you let go of her hand?" Randall's compo-
sure hid his anger.

"Get out of my face, kid. I can talk to this beautiful young lady if I want to. I think she wants to talk to me, too." The man licked his tongue at Jada.

She choked back her disgust and managed to place the tab on the table at last. She attempted to walk away, but the man clung to her hand.

Randall bent down, glaring in the guy's face. "If you don't let go of her hand, I'm going to whip the crap out of you outside."

Jada gawked at Randall because of the threat. "I can handle it, Randall."

"Is this your woman?" the man asked with a smirk. "Well, if I want her, and I do, she will be mine. Kid, you can't compete with me. I can buy and sell you. And I can buy a woman, too. Money talks, kid."

Randall glowered at the jerk until he released Jada's hand. The man left the establishment.

When Jada and Randall exited the restaurant, what they saw slowed their tracks. The man was skulking around in front of the Belvedere.

"Doll, he can't give you what I can," the man taunted. Smug-faced, he leaned against a silver BMW.

Jada hooked her arm around Randall's, steering him toward his Grand Am and away from him. "Come on, baby," she pleaded.

But her words landed on Randall's deaf ears. Seething, he charged in the man's direction. In a flash, he punched the troublemaker in the jaw. The man took a few seconds to recover from the blow, before Randall winced from a jab in the stomach.

Within the span of seconds, Randall was pum-

meling him on the sidewalk. Jada's screams, telling
him this man was not worth it, did not get through
to him. His rage overruled his good sense. He didn't
intend to kill the fool, only to wound him so badly
that he'd wished he had been killed. Nobody disrespected his woman or him. When two men broke
up the brawl, Randall's opponent limped away as
fast as he could. Clutching his ribs, the man wore a
busted lip and a black eye. Randall had minor
bruises and scratches.

At the kitchen window, Ms. Emma glanced out
and saw Jada and Randall strolling toward her house.
She had grown to love them both. Clearly Jada had
been brought up well and had plenty of manners.
Emma observed that she worked hard, too, and
treated people like she wanted to be treated. Randall
made her equally proud.

From her perspective, that boy had always been
a man. His maturity and strength of mind stood
beyond those of any other twenty-year-old she knew.
What's more, Randall was so respectful and always
helped her with chores around the house. She
wasn't surprised at him graduating two years early.
She knew the Lord's hand guided him. She also
knew it would lead him to supreme blessings. Even
so, her love of these young folks did not make her
blind. Jada and Randall had become *too* close.

Adjusting the curtains to ensure that the twosome didn't catch her spying at the window, Emma
noticed they weren't holding hands or hugging.
Despite that, she knew they wanted to. She had
heard the tiptoeing down the hall in the middle of
the night. But what else had she expected of two

young people right down the hall from each other who spent so much time together?

Perhaps if Randall had been in Savannah when Jada visited the college and her home in the spring, she could have detected something in their inter-action that would have made her think twice about letting Jada stay. Nonetheless, Randall had been in Lakeside during that week on spring break. She re-called how disappointed Jada looked.

Emma strode away from the window and took a seat at the table. She never had an ounce of trou-ble with Randall and girls. When his old girlfriend Carolyn came to visit, the young lovers hardly spent any time alone. Mostly they stayed in the liv-ing room listening to records. On other occasions, they barbecued franks and burgers in the back-yard and played cards. Frequently Emma joined them. At nighttime, Carolyn slept in the room Jada now occupied. And Emma never heard any creeping across the hall late at night.

Rules had to be established, she decided at that moment. She had been young once. She knew how two people could be inseparable and dependent on each other, with all these hormones raging. Before you knew it, things could happen. Not in her house.

Moments later, inside Randall's room, Jada stood above him, while he sat on the side of the bed. With a warm cloth, she patted a bruise near his temple.

"You should have just walked away," she scolded in a tender tone.

"No way with him talking all that crap." He an-gled his head, so she could better dab the bruise.

"I bet he won't talk that mess to you again. I laid him out with my fists."

Jada burst out laughing, though she tried hard not to. "Randall, you jacked him up. It was pitiful. I almost felt sorry for the man."

"You like a man who can kick butt, huh?"

She tapped his shoulder. "You're terrible. This is nothing to brag about."

She continued blotting the bruise on his head when suddenly his face pressed into her stomach, kneading it. The pressure aroused that old familiar sensation that she always felt around him. Low in her belly an undeniable craving hit her, weakening every part of her.

"It's getting so hard," he whispered, burying his face deeper into her stomach.

Jada rubbed the back of his head. "I know."

Randall looked up at her. "I want to be with you so badly. I want to be inside you so badly. And I know you want it, too, Jada."

Jada considered his plea. Each time she kissed Randall, she ached for him to strip her until she was bare and make love to her. "I've never done it before."

"You haven't?" he said, trying not to show how excited he was that he would be her first and hopefully her last.

"Not ever."

"I won't hurt you, Jada. You'll be far from hurting."

She smiled shyly. "I know. I know it will be wonderful. But I always wanted to wait until I got married."

"And why is that?" He planted a kiss on her belly.

She tingled and wanted him to do it again. "Because it's the right thing to do and because I was brought up that way. And because of . . ."

"Of what?"

"Love."

"You want to be in love when it happens?"

"Yes."

He stood, looking in her eyes, beholding her heart in them. "You love me, don't you?" He slipped his arms around her waist, drawing her close to him.

"Yes, I love you," she responded, disbelieving that she had confessed what had been within her so long. She knew she loved Randall the first time he kissed her.

"And I love you more than I have ever loved any woman I've been with. And I mean that sincerely."

Jada's heartbeat became fierce. She had never heard him say he loved her, although he always alluded to it. The words, the moment, and Randall, all felt like a beautiful dream. It almost seemed too good to be true.

His lips had just pressed against hers when the door opened, startling them apart.

Witness to the tender scene, Gregory froze. "If I'm interrupting anything, I'll come back later. I just wanted to get my basketball. The fellows and I are going to hit the court."

Jada touched her lips, knowing her lipstick had smeared. "Actually, I was going to my room. I have to call my family. I'll see you later, Randall."

"Most definitely." Trancelike, Randall watched her hips sway as she walked out of the room.

Gregory noted Randall's naughty obsession. He shook his head once they were alone. "You've been getting some of that sweet stuff, haven't you?"

"Get out of here, man." Unable to help smiling, Randall removed the basketball from the closet and tossed it at him. "Now get."

Gregory caught the ball and grinned. "Aw, you've been getting some and it's so good your nose is open."

"What we do is none of your business," Randall said with a laugh. He had come to like Gregory like one of his brothers. Often they sparred playfully on a number of things. "And I'm not telling you anything about Jada."

Amused, Gregory stepped deeper in the room. "You don't have to say nothing. I know. And I don't blame you. Shoot, if I was younger and if my mama wouldn't kill me for trying to date her borders, and of course if you weren't seeing her, I would definitely try to hit on Ms. Jada with her superfine self. She have any older sisters that would go out with me?"

"She has an older sister, but she wouldn't want you," Randall razzed and lightly jabbed Gregory's chubby belly.

Gregory returned the faint blows, but noticed bruises on Randall's forehead and arms. "Hey, man, what happened to you anyway?"

"Had a fight."

"A fight! With who?"

"Some punk who tried to get with Jada and disrespected both of us."

Wildly, Gregory shook his head. "Aw, sookie sookie now. She got the man ready to kill over her. You are done."

"No, I'm not done. I'm just in love with the woman of my dreams." He drifted off in thought,

realizing what he had just uttered aloud to someone other than Jada. But it was his true feeling.

"Aw, shucks," Gregory teased. "She has really, really blown your nose open. In fact, I can see all the
way up into your head."

Jada and Randall couldn't seem to get a moment alone the rest of that evening. If Ms. Emma
didn't have her helping with the dinner or fixing
the drapes, Mr. Winston had Randall outside with
him tinkering with his old Cadillac.

Hence, the following day Jada and Randall
couldn't wait to be alone. It was Friday, Randall's
early day for leaving work. Jada's shift finished
early as well. When he picked her up from the
restaurant, they drove out to his favorite secluded
place. Only this time, there wasn't any food and
neither cared about the sumptuous scenery. As
soon as Randall spread out his blanket on the
grass, he steered Jada down on it backward.

"Can I make love to you, Jada?" He lay beside
her and propped himself up on his elbow. Leaning
over her, he gazed down in her face. Her fear and
desire had caused little droplets to sprinkle across
her forehead. He pecked them all away.

"I want to, Randall, so bad. But I'm scared."

"Don't be scared."

Randall rubbed her hair, then her cheeks, lips,
neck, and at last her chest just above her breasts.
Quivers of anticipation vibrated from her body to
his. He kissed her gently, then more greedily. Jada
responded, tasting him hungrily and bringing her
arms around his back.

Powerless against the sexual tension, Randall rose up. His eyes locked in on Jada's eyes, he removed his shirt, tie, and undershirt.

Moist, bronzed, sweat-glazed, muscular chest and arms glistened at Jada. "Randall, you're so beautiful," she said, gliding her palm along his arms and chest.

"You're beautiful, too, baby." He held her face and stared at it silently.

Arousal building within Jada caused her legs to weaken. "I think I'm ready."

"Don't worry, baby," Randall assured her. He bent down, touching her chest again. Yet he dared to go lower. Randall unbuttoned her blouse and felt her trembling with each inch of flesh that became revealed. When he finally had the top completely undone, Randall opened it widely, nearly slipping it off her shoulders. Bare, full, luscious breasts were exposed to him. He drew in a breath. Jada hadn't worn a bra. Randall hardened a thousand times more than he ever had. "You don't know how many times I imagined you like this."

"You did?" she asked, loving the way he looked at her body.

"You're sexier than I had ever imagined. Oh, baby . . . I can't wait."

Randall's tongue thrust past her lips at the same moment his fingertips feathered upon her pebble-hard nipples. His hands on her felt so good that rockets of pleasure raised her slightly from the blanket. She arched her chest forward for him to do more.

He heard her hot-blooded cry and replied with his lips kissing her entire breast and soon laving his tongue around them. Jada could feel the ecstasy building in her lower body and dripping out of her. Loudly she moaned and reached down in his pants. His rock-hard loving shocked and thrilled her. She stroked him, making him breathe heavier than he already was. She also wondered how it was going to feel with all of Randall's manhood melted within her. He felt so thick and long.

Was she actually touching him this way? Was she actually going to be with a man for the first time? Was that man going to be Randall? The Randall she had desired for so long?

"Oh, Jada, baby, keep doing that," he whispered huskily into her silky breasts. "You know how to please me."

Randall raised his mouth to hers, but kept his hands on her soft roundness. He was on fire. He had never been so turned on. If he didn't feel the sweetness between those honeyed thighs soon, his loving would burst all over her.

Kissing her harder, he reached beneath her skirt. Her satiny thighs were warm, even warmer on the inner skin. Randall felt himself harden more.

"Jada," he slurred between their mouths. "What are you doing to me, baby?"

Randall kissed her deeper and raised his hand to reach her panties and caress her wet softness. Rustling within nearby bushes was all that interrupted their passion. Randall sprang up, looking in the direction of the noise.

Jada joined him, while quickly buttoning her blouse. A dog, sniffing the ground, made his way toward them. His owner trekked in their direction, too. Jada rushed to neaten her clothes.

"No, not now!" Randall snapped. "Since when did anybody come out here? Talk about bad luck!"

Jada hurried up on her feet and reached down for his hand. "Randall, we better go. That man sees us. He might tell somebody we're out here having sex and we might get arrested or something."

"You're right, baby," he said with an annoyed sigh. "Let's go home. Maybe we can find some privacy there."

Privacy didn't come until the next afternoon when Ms. Emma, Mr. Winston, and Mr. Harrell headed out to City Market to go grocery shopping. As soon as Mr. Harrell's Lincoln pulled out of the driveway, Jada entered Randall's bedroom.

Without uttering a word, he clung to her on his bed, kissing her, his hands reacquainting themselves with her soft flesh. A knock at the partly open door interrupted him just as he was about to undress her. Randall jumped up and stood by the window, faking that he peered out of it.

Jada hopped over in the cushy old chair far across the room and brushed her hair down neatly with her fingers.

"Randall?" Ms. Emma said through the door. "Can I come in, son?"

"Any time you want."

Stern-faced, she sauntered into the room. She looked at both of them for a moment before crossing her arms over her chest. "I was headed to the market when I remembered that a man was coming by to fix the washing machine and I forgot to tell you, Randall. But Lord, I sure had an eyeful through the crack of this bedroom door."

Jada dropped her head.

Randall's lips moved, but nothing came out of his mouth.

"Now, Randall, you know I love you like my own grandchild," Ms. Emma stated.

"Well, I have three grandmothers as far as I'm concerned," Randall told her, "and the third is you." He winked at her.

Ms. Emma ignored the wink, a sign of affection he often bestowed upon her. Her gray-brown eyes then found Jada. "And, Jada, I haven't known you long. But you're like one of my own, too."

"Ms. Emma, I feel the same way about you."

"I'm glad to hear all this," Ms. Emma went on. "But I'm not glad to see what I just saw."

Jada and Randall glanced at each other.

"Here I am, about to walk in here, and I see you two wrapped up together like a ball of yarn. I am very disappointed. Randall, after all these years of knowing me, you should know I don't allow *that* in my house. Not sex without the blessing of marriage. And, Jada, if you don't know it, I'm telling you right now.

"I've been planning to talk to ya'll about the house rules, but it made me uncomfortable, so I put it off. I see now that I shouldn't have. I know at this age your hormones are all out of whack and driving you crazy and stuff. I was young, too. I know that sometimes you feel like you're going to jump out of your skin. But there will be no jumping out of your skin together up in here. Do I make myself clear?"

"Yes, Ms. Emma," Jada mumbled.

"We apologize, Ms. Emma," Randall added.

"I appreciate that. Because I'm no tattletale. I would hate to pick up the phone, Randall, and call your mama and tell her to come and calm you down before she becomes a grandmama. And I don't want to do that to you either, Jada. You two got me so upset that I don't even want to go out anymore. I'll tell Mr. Winston and Mr. Harrell to go without me." Ms. Emma marched out of the room.

In silence, Randall looked at Jada. After a second, he walked over to her. Grasping her hands, he kissed her on the lips softly.

Jada pulled back, shaking her head. "Randall, you heard what Ms. Emma said. You better watch that in the house."

"I know what we say. We want each other. We love each other."

She loved to hear him say that, but she was still worried. "I don't want to get in trouble."

"We won't. We can go to a hotel. But we might not have to. Tomorrow Ms. Emma's going to church and you know she's there all day. Mr. Winston and Mr. Harrell usually go with her, too."

Jada smiled. "Ooh, Randall, you're sneaky."

"We'll have the whole house to ourselves. We'll have all day to make love."

On Sunday, Jada and Randall were frustrated when Ms. Emma and her boarders skipped the morning service. Fortunately, they decided to attend the afternoon Pastor's Anniversary celebration. Once Mr. Winston's car roared off down the street, Randall raised his fist in the air and cheered, "Yes!" Hurriedly, his bare feet thumped against the cool wooden floor en route to Jada's room.

He pushed the door open. Jada lay sprawled across the bed in a lilac satin nightgown.

"Wow!" he exclaimed, shaking his head.

"I bought it at the mall yesterday after our close call. I wanted to look special for you today."

"You always look special to me."

Randall joined her on the bed, wrapping her in his arms. He savored the suppleness of her body and drank in the addictive smell of it, too. She always exuded a fruity scent. It seemed like a potpourri of peach, strawberry, and watermelon. Randall's body was ready for hers, more ready than he ever knew his body could be. Yet he knew there was something he had to do before they went a step further.

After coaxing her head against his chest, he revealed, "I'm planning to stay in Savannah and not return home in the fall."

Jada rose up to look at him carefully. "You are? When did you decide this?"

Down the hallway, in Randall's bedroom, the phone rang. They ignored it.

Randall pecked her lips. "I can't leave you and go back home in the fall like I planned. Since I met you I want to stay at my job past the summer and I'm looking at real estate here in Savannah. I figure I can work there awhile, save up, and buy property here. And then when you graduate, we'll decide our next steps. Maybe we might want to stay here in Savannah. Maybe we might want to go to Lakeside, or maybe to Jersey around your family. And I can buy property anywhere, and I will—lots of it—so I can take you out and treat you like a queen. And I also want to help you get that bookstore you always wanted."

The telephone stopped ringing and started again.

His words immersed her in a dreamy mist. He loved her so much that he planned to make drastic changes in his plans to be with her. "Randall, you sure you want to do this?"

"Of course I'm sure. I want to be with you. I *have* to be with you and I have to make sure you're well taken care of. Because I plan to be with you forever."

Jada knew what she heard, but she couldn't believe it. "I want to be with you forever, too."

The phone persisted in ringing and then stopped.

They kissed. All over her smoldering flesh, his lips wandered insatiably, even caressing her thighs and soon tugging at her lacy bikini panties.

"Randall? Randall?" The intrusive, panicked male voice called. Mr. Harrell knocked repeatedly. "Randall, are you in there?"

Randall nearly cursed as he sat up. The old man had stayed behind to ruin his love life.

Jada's heart went up in her throat. Not knowing what to do, she bit her lip and tidied herself.

"Randall, if you're in there, your phone kept ringing, so I answered it. It's your family, son. There's trouble at home."

Randall tore out of the room, rushing past Mr. Harrell. When he returned, Mr. Harrell and Jada were concerned by the dazed look on his face.

"Randall, what's wrong?" Jada asked, coming over to him. She held his face. "Did something happen to someone in your family?"

"Son, what's wrong?" Mr. Harrell pressed.

"It's, uh . . . it's Carolyn," Randall replied, his gaze scattering about the floor. "She, uh, was in a car accident. They say she's badly injured and might not make it and she's asking for me. I have to go home. I have to go now."

The moments went by in a blur for Jada. Ms. Emma and Mr. Winston were home by the time Randall kissed Jada good-bye. As he bent down to get in his car, he promised to call. He promised that he would be back soon. Soon after, he drove off.

Jada watched his car until it vanished in the distance. Mixed emotions ripped her apart. On the one hand, she prayed that Carolyn would be all right. On the other hand, she wished that she hadn't asked for Randall. They weren't involved anymore. Why couldn't Carolyn just leave him alone, so she could have his love forever like they planned? Why was something telling her she would never see him again?

Ms. Emma gazed over at Jada. Her young boarder gazed at the street where Randall had just driven his car from. Tears rolled down her cheeks and Ms. Emma couldn't help putting her arms around her. Yes, she had come down hard on the young lovers about fornicating in her house. Still, she knew they truly loved each other. She saw it. She *felt* it.

"Don't worry, darling," she said, patting Jada's shoulder. "There's something that I've heard all my life. First heard grown folks saying it when I was barely able to talk. Didn't know what it meant then, but God knows I know now. And that is if someone really, really loves you, and you're meant to be together, somehow, or someway, they will come into your life again. It may not happen when you want. It may not happen the *way* you want. It may not happen until years and years and years from now, but if it's meant to be, you will be part of each other's lives again in this lifetime."

Chapter Two

January 2004

Jada dipped her curves in a potpourri of fruit-scented bath bubbles, hoping that soaking in the warmth would ease her worry away. Only a few weeks engaged and she ached because the one man who never hurt her had been gone from his condominium too long. Possessiveness wasn't her style. Her hubby-to-be had the right to enjoy moments without her and vice versa. But Michael had left over three hours ago.

A nearby bakery was his destination. He wanted to spoil her with her new favorite dessert, banana flambé. Twenty minutes was the longest time it should have taken him.

Laying her head back against the tub, Jada closed her mink-colored eyes and her wild imagination scurried into overdrive with somber thoughts. She prayed that harm hadn't come to Michael this evening. It had taken too long to find him.

Shortly after graduation from Savannah State, she married her college boyfriend, Derrick. For six years they enjoyed each other. Everything changed when misery stormed through Jada's family. Her brother-in-law did horrible things to her sister, Katherine, causing her older sibling to suffer a nervous breakdown.

A mental facility became Katherine's temporary residence. Her husband abandoned their four children. Worsening Jada's family turbulence, her mother ran back and forth from the hospital with complications from high blood pressure. Her grandmother suffered from arthritis.

Taking care of her big sister's four big babies until she recovered was an undertaking Jada felt she had to do. The children had always felt like her babies, too. Her husband, Derrick, adored them as well.

Jada and he discussed temporary guardianship. Derrick welcomed the idea of taking the youngsters into their home. After all, Jada had always been there to lend a hand to his troubled family. The greatest sacrifice had been giving Derrick money she had saved to open her bookstore, so together their funds could save his mother from losing her house. Derrick promised to replace the money for her dream.

But after having her nephews and nieces as houseguests for merely three months, Derrick resented them. The kids acted politely, respectfully, did their homework, and performed chores around the house voluntarily. Overall, they were mature, well-behaved children. That meant little to Derrick.

He yelled at them for the most trivial matters.

Whenever he did it, Jada's wrath came down on him hard. Constantly he complained about a lack of privacy and the financial burden these youngsters put on their household. Jada argued back that she cared for them with *her* earnings, not his. Besides, she hadn't complained about the large amounts of money his siblings had borrowed from them and never paid back. Neither did she hound him about the savings for her bookstore, which had not been replaced.

After a while, Derrick claimed that he hated coming home. To underscore that statement, he stayed away from their house often. Then that day came when he arranged a meeting at their home with a couple seeking to adopt, whom he barely knew. Jada had no idea about the meeting until the day the folks lounged in her living room. Derrick proposed that they take Katherine's children.

Livid, Jada escorted the people out of her house and threatened to leave Derrick. Derrick left her instead. Days later, he returned.

With each new day, he pressed her to choose between the children or him. But not even his hard-heartedness had dulled the love she felt for him. She knew he had married her—not her nieces and nephews. Even so, when they had taken their marriage vows, supporting each other through hardships were part of that oath before God. She had supported him. He balked at those vows, determined to kick her sister's children into the street—and hand them to strangers.

So how could she feel secure living the rest of her life with a man capable of such coldness? When something unpleasant or discomforting occurred, would he kick her out, too? When life became challenging and harsh and wasn't fun, would he do a disappearing act? Men had already done it to her grandmother, mother, and Katherine.

Derrick's actions toward the children screamed the answer. Until this moment, she hadn't known his true soul. No way would she let him throw helpless children wherever the wind blew them. Added to it all, they soon stopped communicating. Respect and tenderness vanished. Passion didn't exist anymore. Quarrels were all that existed between them. Eventually they divorced.

Other men had crossed Jada's path since that time. Not all of them were terrible either. Yet each man had showed her that true, unconditional love rarely graced one's life in these modern days. Either that, or sadly, it wasn't meant for her.

Then Michael came. Jaw-droppingly handsome, he owned the auto mechanic shop she passed during her trek to work each day at Kessman Realty. Two years of an odyssey packed with fun, kindness, and respect had culminated in a proposal on New Year's Eve. That day was also her thirty-eighth birthday.

Jada hadn't felt this happy in a long time . . . not since she spent that unforgettable summer with Randall. But after what happened, she had come to realize that those magical moments she experienced during that time had likely been one-sided.

Outside the bathroom, the click of the door opening made Jada sit up so fast and hard the water swished like loud slaps. "Michael?" she called anxiously. "Is that you?"

"Yeah, it's me, baby."

Exhaling a relieved breath, Jada hurried out of the tub. The pearly, marble tile felt cold against her feet as she reached for a brass rack that held her towels. Swiftly she patted the warm droplets on her skin and snuggled a dry, thigh-length towel around her body. Barefoot, she padded out onto the rust-carpeted living room.

Michael's appearance stopped her short. Perspiration drenched his rich brown complexion. His curly hair looked messy. Odder, when he took off his leather bomber, his blue jogging suit appeared disheveled.

Jada's rounded jaw dropped. "What in the world happened to you? And you're sweating in this cold weather?"

Michael rested a silver bag on an end table and then wiped across his slick forehead. "After I left the bakery, I—I looked in a few stores and then went jogging. Guess I'll hop in the shower now." Rotating his shoulders as if they were stiff, he stepped toward the bathroom. "I saw some real nice things for you. But I didn't have enough cash on me and I couldn't find my credit cards. I must have left them here."

Smelling the hot, brandied, banana aroma wafting from the bag, Jada felt her taste buds begging for the delicacy. Even so, her hunger had to wait. Michael's answers hadn't satisfied her. She could even have understood if he had said that he stopped by his ex-wife's house to see his kids. His son and daughter lived fifteen minutes away.

Jada's bare feet crushed into the thick carpet, making a slightly lighter trail to the bathroom. When she reached the door, she felt funny. Michael had closed it.

He always loved to leave the door open and tease her with his awesomely built body. More erotic, he loved to yank her into the shower, strip her, and thrill her with hot-blooded love beneath the stream. "You spent all that time looking in stores and jogging?" she yelled at him through the door. "Michael, I was worrying like crazy about you!" She heard her high pitch and softened her voice. "Do you realize how long you were gone?"

Swiping a stray, lengthy hair off her cheekbone, Jada listened for his response. Hearing nothing for a long while, she heard the door suddenly crack open.

Michael stuck solely his head and shoulders out. His deep-set eyes flashed anger. "My goodness, Jada! Is it going to be like this now? I go off alone for a little while and you fly off the handle. Good grief!"

Jada swayed back. Her concern riling him so much amazed her. "I'm sorry," she apologized, not because she meant it, but to sustain the peace. "I just love you and thought something awful might have happened. That's all."

Michael's expression lightened. "I'm sorry, too, baby. I didn't mean to go off. I guess I just have to get used to the idea of being married again after being a bachelor for the last three years." A wide set of piano-straight teeth gleamed at her. "I have to give up doing things spontaneously, like just goofing off for a few hours." He stretched his head out a smidgen more and pecked her on the forehead. The door closed soon after.

Jada picked up her bag with the flambé off the table and roamed into the dining room with the strangest feeling. She tried to shake it off. Except that voice inside her kept whispering, *Something isn't right.*

Jada's strong sense of something awry continued that night. Michael behaved restlessly. Evidently something preoccupied him. Several times, Jada asked him if something was wrong. Each time he responded with a peck on her lips and professed, "I'm just tired after all that running."

When she attempted to engage him in conversation about the wedding plans or her anxiety about all the downsizing at her job, Michael half listened. More than once, Jada felt so ignored she started to go home. Perhaps this was one of those weekends that he preferred being with his kids.

In the midst of a cable movie they watched, Michael cut off the television unexpectedly. At last he appeared as if he wanted to get something off his chest. Rather than talking, though, he pulled Jada up from the sofa and guided her to his bedroom. Once they reached the room, he kissed her feverishly.

Among his cologne-drenched sheets, Jada pushed her agonizing aside. She took pleasure in the steamy foreplay Michael always indulged her with. Nonetheless, each time her fingers drifted along his back, she received a bizarre reaction. Michael would steer her hands to another part of his body. She thought it was peculiar and felt his back anyway. Scratches she felt threw her heart up in her throat.

She sprang back from him. "Why do you have scratches on your back? I never scratch you. I don't have long nails." Her mind had a flash of a pair of long red nails she had seen from time to time.

Michael lowered his head, his palm clutching his eyes. "I'm confused."

"What is that supposed to mean? What does that have to do with those scratches on your back?" Her chest heaved from what her good sense told her, but it couldn't be. Her Michael would not devastate her. Not him.

He gazed up. "I don't want to be confused, but this is how I feel. I can't help it."

"Michael, what is going on?"

"I've really screwed everything up tonight."

Red nails flashed again—the red nails that belonged to his ex-wife. "Were you *with* Vanessa?"

Michael looked off, then back at her. "I thought I would just drop by to see my kids for a minute. They wanted some extra money to go bowling. I gave it to them. Vanessa was driving them to the bowling alley and she offered to drive me back here. On our way here, she started talking about my engagement to you."

"What about our engagement?"

"She thinks . . ."

Jada sat up straight. "She thinks what?"

"That I'm making a mistake. She said she never stopped loving me and we should give it another try, especially for my son and daughter's sake. She says that my daughter just cries about my marrying you all the time. And it's bothering my son so much that his grades are getting screwed up."

"And what did you say to this?"

"Of course I told her how much I love you."

Jada fought back a fullness of emotion wedged

in her throat. It strangled her words, but she still managed to ask, "But the love didn't stop something from happening tonight, right? Did you have sex with her?"

Michael gazed across the room. "I'm sorry, so, so sorry."

Jada's heart joined in the assault on her, pounding up in her ears and head. She started to rock to tame the scream fighting to leap out. "Where did it happen?" She hated knowing, but she had to know. "Where did this happen?" she shouted.

Michael gazed at her silently. "She parked in this out-of-the-way area we used to drive to and she kissed me in the car . . . and . . ."

"So it happened in the car? All that sweat from jogging was really sweat from *screwing* your ex-wife in the car?"

"It wasn't just screwing. We have children together."

"So your bodies should automatically fit together when you see each other?"

"Jada, I'm confused. I know I love you, but . . ."

"But what, Michael?"

He frowned. "I'm going to have to give it another try with Vanessa. I have to do what's right for my kids. Maybe I won't feel confused anymore. The kids come first. Certainly as much as you love your nieces and nephews and have just about given up your life for them, you of all people should understand why I am making this decision."

Jada returned to her apartment that evening. She slung her coat on the couch, kicked off her shoes, and lugged her exhausted limbs straight to bed. Slumber mocked her cruelly for the countless moments she lay in the dark with her eyes wide open.

All the love she had given Michael wasn't enough. All that she was wasn't enough. She had completed the curse of the women in her family. A man had deserted her grandmother and mother. A man had even deserted her sister and stolen her sanity. Now a man deserted her—once again.

If Jada had called her family and told them about the broken engagement at this very moment, her mother and grandmother would have urged her to be strong like they had been. Yet she pondered how strong they really were during their private moments, when their hearts had been ripped out. It all gave her this strange feeling of emptiness.

Every way Jada turned, a bellyache of emptiness hit her. With every piece of cover that she touched or covered herself with, the emptiness lingered and the pain worsened. Despite everything she tried to think about to make herself feel better, the reality of Michael no longer wanting her crept up over it, and the emptiness and pain were all there was. The hurt was inside, all around her, and everywhere. How could she make it stop?

Oh God, here I am again all alone, she thought, closing her eyes tight, trying to shut the tears out. Still, they began to flow. *He doesn't want me anymore. He doesn't love me anymore. Nobody is ever going to love me.*

When the tears became too much for her, Jada felt her shoulders shake. Raw screams roared through the air. But she couldn't stop them. At one point, she sat up, believing she was about to vomit or even die. Nothing had hurt this bad since she was eighteen. That's when she learned that Randall had lied.

To assuage her anguish in the coming months, Jada buried herself in her work at Kessman Realty. For years, she had worked in different areas of real estate while secretly planning to open her bookstore one day. She dreamed of setting the bookstore up and making it a wonderland for patrons. Once that was accomplished, she longed to explore other entrepreneurial projects and buy some property of her own. Randall had piqued her interest in real estate. Randall had intrigued her with many things.

Due to her helping loved ones, her most heart-felt dreams got shoved further and further away. Currently, she worked as an industrial and office broker. What she hadn't counted on, nevertheless, was the deteriorating economy. Downsizing that had overtaken her company during the past year finally knocked on her door one day.

"Jada, you're a treasure," her boss, Mr. Kessman, said entering her cubicle with reddened eyes. "So it tears me up to say this, but I'm going to have to let you go for a while. You know how the economy is right now. Companies are closing and people are hesitant to start up new companies and have that rent overhead. When things pick back up, you'll be the first one I call."

Jada had prayed that her job loss was temporary as her employer implied. She learned otherwise. With the weeks of joblessness turning into months and her having no stable income, she grew desper-

ate. By the first of July, her rent had fallen behind.
In addition, the house her mother, sister, and grandmother
shared needed costly repairs. Her niece also
needed money for college. She had received financial
aid and a small loan. Still, more money was
needed for a portion of the tuition.

Jada's mother, grandmother, and her sister, Katherine,
had no means of coming up with the money
for the repairs or tuition. Because of her high blood
pressure, her mother needed a stress-free lifestyle,
healthful eating, exercise, and rest, and couldn't
work. Her grandmother had retired early from the
post office because of her arthritis and lived on a
fixed income.

As for Katherine, who had once been a nurse,
she had never fully recovered from her breakdown.
Periodically she battled depression and disliked
going outside or being around strangers,
especially men. She received outpatient psychiatric
care and disability benefits.

Obsessed with helping her family, Jada sent out
hundreds of resumes to land a job. She pounded
the pavement and went on countless interviews for
a variety of positions in real estate. She even applied
for sales trainee and office assistant, two positions
that she first sank her heels in in this
profession. The "we'll call you" speech she heard
over and over again.

At last, Jada swallowed her pride. She turned to
friends, letting them know how desperately she
sought work. Maybe one of their friends or relatives
had a position open, or knew of someone
who did.

When she phoned Kelly one afternoon, it was as
if a prayer had been answered.

"My uncle has just opened up new, luxury villas in St. Thomas," Kelly informed her, "and he needs a property manager ASAP."

"You're kidding me."

"No, I'm not. Jay, your timing is perfect. The qualified applicant will get a hefty salary and I believe a rent-free, furnished villa. And Uncle Nelson is easy to work with, too. So what do you say?"

"Girl, you know I couldn't turn down a chance like this. I've never been to St. Thomas, but I know enough about it to know that it's just what I need right now—an island paradise to help me get over all the drama I've had to deal with these past months."

"You're right about that. St. Thomas will sure take away the blues. I went there many times and came back feeling like a new woman. And I know once my uncle interviews you, he will think you're perfect for the position."

"I hope so. With my luck . . ."

"Oh, Jay, think positive. Just let me set everything up over the phone with my uncle and you just pack your bags and get ready to fly down to a tropical paradise."

"Could you ask him if there are any licensing requirements?"

"Sure. I'll hook you up. And maybe I'll hook you up with even more than a new job. Who knows? Maybe you'll meet a cutie down there."

"*Please.* A man is the last thing on my mind. I just need a job, and, girl, you are the best friend a person could have for looking out for me like this. Thank you so much."

"You know I'd do anything for you," Kelly said

and raised her sparkly, hazel eyes to the heavens. She hoped God would forgive her for the few fibs she told. But it was only because she loved Jada like a sister and knew exactly what she needed.

When Jada hung up the telephone, she felt hopeful. Having worked in property management before, she felt more than qualified for the position. She also loved the idea of working and residing in a place as exotic as St. Thomas. If it turned out to be the tropical paradise everyone claimed it was, then maybe she could convince her family to relocate.

The more she thought about it, the more she started getting a good feeling about it. Once again, Kelly had looked out for her. She had to send her a nice thank-you gift.

For a second, it crossed her mind that Randall might be working with his uncle, since both of them owned real estate. Nonetheless, Kelly would have mentioned Randall's association with the venture. She understood how much Randall had hurt her and knew she avoided ever seeing him again.

After Randall broke her heart years ago, Kelly and she still remained friends over the years. They attended sorority conventions, took trips together, and called each other several times throughout the year.

However, Jada never accepted invitations to the Larimore home in Lakeside, Virginia, no matter what the celebration. Running into Randall again would have been unbearable even after all these years. He made it clear how he felt about her. If his uncle hired her, she hoped Randall wasn't going to visit him in St. Thomas any time soon.

Chapter Three

Palm trees swayed against the St. Thomas skyline like fluttering angel's wings. Gazing up from the limousine's window while coasting along the Larimore estate, Jada viewed such a sight as a sign of something wonderful to come. Hopefully when Kelly's uncle, Nelson Larimore, interviewed her for the property management position for his new luxury villas, her qualifications would convince him to hire her on the spot.

She had already fallen in love with St. Thomas's scenic capital, Charlotte Amalie. Emerald hills, crystal waters, and a brilliant blue sky looked more striking than they did in the travel brochures. Easily she pictured her mother, sister, and grandmother lounging on the lawn in front of a magnificent house. Sipping tropical drinks, they would take pleasure in cackling and watching the kids running around playing games.

The limousine stopped in front of the Larimore mansion, nudging Jada from her flight of imagination. The neatly dressed driver helped her out of the vehicle, into the heat that the car's air conditioner shielded her from. She tripped because of her preoccupation with the scenery. The light beige brick mansion, trimmed in white, had a rectangular appearance. Its three floors perched on acres of manicured grass. Bright red, yellow, white, pink, orange, and lavender roses intermingled stunningly with a multitude of palm trees that adorned the land. A turquoise sea behind the property made the panorama dreamy.

"This is so beautiful," she thought aloud.

"Yes, it is, ma'am," the driver agreed in a delightful accent and with a huge smile.

Afterward he rang the doorbell. A maid instructed him to escort Jada to a patio on the side of the house to wait to be interviewed. He followed her directions and wished Jada a splendid day.

Jada relaxed at a round white table with an umbrella crowning it. Inhaling mowed grass, she gazed in the distance at the ocean. *What a life Nelson Larimore has,* she thought.

If she resided in such a breathtaking place, she wouldn't want much else. On the other hand, if she was hired for this position with its excellent salary, a home like this could be part of her future, Jada contemplated further; that is, if she also pursued her dream to open a bookstore and later explore other business opportunities. Sharing a house this perfect with her family would be sheer joy. However, no way in the world would she share it with a man.

Since Michael had deceived her into believing he was the love of her life, Jada mistrusted her judgment about the opposite sex. If, or, when, she decided to date again, men would be her companions and nothing more. The betrayal had even affected her physical attraction to men. Since her split with Michael, not one man had given her the slightest buzz of female desire.

Jada reflected about Michael for several minutes when suddenly movement from behind distracted her. Strangely the presence caused fluttering in her belly. She hadn't experienced that sensation since that summer so long ago.

Trembling and not understanding why, Jada twisted around in her seat to see who had walked up behind her. She gasped. At the same instant, her eyes stretched, looking up into the face of the tall, powerfully built man standing above her. She didn't know whether it was the shock of who he was, or that he was so much more muscular than he was many years before. Whatever it was, her heart knocked against her chest like never before. Breath caught in her throat. Somehow sounds and sights around them faded.

Jada stood. Her awareness of him grew potent as he came nearer. Smoldering eyes, whose compelling stare could always seduce her mind and her body, held hers. They invited her to roam lower. There she beheld lips that bared a naturally flirtatious curl—lips that she knew the sensual taste of well. Stronger fluttering hit the bottom of her stomach and she fought to repossess her lost voice.

"Randall?"

Shocked at setting eyes on Jada again, Randall needed a few seconds to acknowledge her calling his name. "Yes, it's me, Jada. I can't believe I'm seeing you again either."

His raging heartbeat shook his entire body.

Randall studied her face quietly, noticing that her eyes were still sexier than sin. It was something about the way that she always looked at him that got to him even then. It was something about *her* that made him feel like a young boy again, wanting and wanting like he never wanted before.

Her hairstyle looked different from the simple, straight way she used to wear it. Now wild, wavy brown hair skimmed her shoulders. Her plump lips glistened with peach gloss. Fixated on them, he recalled her addictive taste so much that he swallowed with hunger.

Randall swallowed again. He couldn't help himself in easing his interest lower to the swell of caramel-coated cleavage exposed from the V neckline of her white silk top. Memories of her being bare from the waist up made him swallow again. Neither could he stop his gaze from falling to her hips, which were rounder than he remembered.

Oh my God, he groaned within. Raw hot-bloodedness gripped him, making his entire body feel as if it were stone. Yet it didn't embarrass him away from pulling Jada within his arms for a gigantic hug.

"It's *so* good to see you after all these years. It's *so, so* good."

Good hardly described how Jada felt within Randall's embrace. She reached up to his broad shoulders and clung to his hard body in return. It all felt so delicious, she almost didn't care that he had walked out of Ms. Emma's house twenty years ago, calling her only once and writing only once. She never heard from him or saw him again.

When she pressured Kelly about what had prevented Randall from returning to her or contacting her, his sister hesitated discussing his situation. At last, she shared that Randall stayed at Carolyn's hospital bedside day and night during her critical condition. His devotion continued after she recovered enough to return home.

During her lengthy recuperation, Carolyn and Randall resumed their relationship. Jada almost failed her classes thinking about them—and him. From the time she woke each day until she went to bed, Randall obsessed her. Above all, Jada questioned if he had loved her. It took a year for her to accept that his "I love you" had truly been "I lust for you."

Now they stood holding each other. Life had surprised her once again.

When they unclasped themselves, Jada's head still spun from his magnetism. It amazed her. After all these years, Randall shouldn't have been able to make her heart pound madly. He shouldn't have caused her legs to feel as weak as they did at that moment. He shouldn't have made her feel suddenly sensually awakened. Above all, after all these years, she shouldn't have even entertained memories of long ago, the bitter or the sweet.

"It's nice seeing you, too, Randall. But I don't understand. I was supposed to be interviewing with your uncle Nelson for the property management position for the luxury villas. I had no idea you would be here."

Randall half smiled and half frowned. "So you're the one? Kelly set up an interview with me for the position and told me that an old friend of hers from Lakeside was coming to the interview. She said she wanted to surprise me and that the person was extremely qualified and I would be pleased. For a second you crossed my mind, but she insisted it wasn't you. She indicated that the person lived in Lakeside with us throughout childhood and I believed her. That girl lied to me. She lied good, too."

Jada mulled over Kelly's mischief. "Well, she kept something from me. She didn't tell me that you would be here interviewing with your uncle Nelson."

"I have news for you, Jada. Kelly lied to you, too. I'm the majority owner of the villas. They are new. I've been living here a little over a month and I'm the only one doing the interviewing for the property management position. Uncle Nelson threw in some funds as an extra retirement investment. He has none of the hands-on work here. My uncle still lives in Lakeside, fishing all day. I can't even get him to come here, he loves Virginia so much."

"But the driver . . . I told him I was going to Nelson Larimore's estate and he said he knew the place."

"That's because in honor of my uncle, I call it Nelson Larimore's estate. The islanders call it that or the Larimore estate." Shaking his head, Randall smiled at her.

Jada shared his amusement. "Kelly, she . . ."

"Set us up. She's matchmaking." Randall laughed until he noticed that Jada wasn't anymore. She appeared somber. "You're not comfortable with the idea of working with me?"

"I'm . . . I'm fine with it . . . really."

He looked unsure if she told the truth. "How have you been?"

"Fine."

"And your family?"

"Everyone's fine. And I know yours is, too. Kelly keeps me updated. I wanted to come to Jackson's wedding."

"So what stopped you?"

She couldn't tell him it was the fear of seeing him again. She shrugged her shoulders. "I was busy."

"I would have loved to see you there."

Tense silence trailed those words and Jada felt uncomfortable. For Randall stared at her openly.

"I'm so happy that your dad is doing great with his gourmet dessert business," she said, trying to lighten the mood. "Kelly has been sending me every new dessert that comes out. They are delicious."

"Aren't they? They make your toes wiggle they are so good."

They chuckled together.

Still, Randall noticed sadness about her.

"And of course, Kelly updated me on your tremendous success," she mentioned. "Congratulations, Randall. You always were hard and were a determined person. I knew you would make your dreams come true."

Her words touched him deeply. "Thank you. But I'd like to update you on me. More importantly, I'd like to catch up with what's been going on in your life."

"Fine," she said, disbelieving they were this close to each other again. She wasn't prepared for this and she wished Kelly hadn't played Cupid. "I think we better get on with the interview."

Randall studied her quietly again. She appeared guarded. Why couldn't they just take their time getting reacquainted again? Then again, it had been twenty years since they looked in each other's eyes. So much had probably happened in her life to change her. Certainly so much had gone on in his.

They sat across from each other at the patio table. While she searched throughout her attaché case for her resume, she felt Randall's gaze raking over her. Once she handed her credentials to him, she couldn't tame her own fascination with him.

Against a velvety Caribbean-tan complexion, black silken goatee hairs framed his lusciously flirtatious mouth. He had gained about ten pounds and it was all muscle. And when he looked up, he still had that way of staring at her that made her feel as if he sent her a secret suggestive message. The message was all in her head this time, she assured herself.

"I'm very impressed with your resume," Randall stated, dividing his attention between her and the two-page document. "I see that you've really done a lot in real estate. Years ago you were undecided about what field to get into for a nine-to-five, although you knew you wanted to have a bookstore one day."

She was surprised he remembered about the bookstore or her indecision about where she first wanted to work. "Well, uh . . . you piqued my interest in real estate," she admitted. "And I like it a lot."

"Good," he said, staring at her and then forcing his attention back on the document. "You are certainly qualified for this position. And I really need a sharp, knowledgeable person who can handle many of the responsibilities with this real estate venture. Many of the villas are still being built on the land and I have to oversee much of the construction and many other properties that I own in

Lakeside and other places, along with constantly seeking investments. And some tell me I shouldn't do it, but I assist with the building and even do repairs on my properties, simply because I enjoy it." He smiled. "So your background would be invaluable to me getting this property properly managed."

Randall went on to inform Jada of what the position entailed. He discussed the benefits, such as various types of insurance plans. As well, he told her about a rent-free, furnished villa that his property manager would reside in. Additionally, he outlined what he expected of her.

Listening and observing him, Jada was stunned by Randall's transformation into business mode. He proceeded to conduct the interview by grilling her with difficult questions and even expressing that he had planned to hire a person with more years of experience than she had. At one point, she believed he wasn't going to hire her. Only after driving her to see the villas, touring the lavish properties, and showing her her likely residence, he offered her the position.

"Thank you so much, Randall. I really needed this job. And I will give it my all. I'm fine with the relocation and I don't expect any special treatment because we were . . ."

"In love." He finished her sentence, staring in her eyes.

As if he cast a spell on her, Jada was drawn to the lingering look until she realized she could have given him the wrong impression. All she needed from Randall was a job.

"I'm hoping we will have a long, productive association," he said with a clearing of his throat. "Now, when can you start?"

"I have to take care of some of my affairs back home. And I do want to spend the Fourth of July with my family. So I can start right after the holiday."

"Great. What time does your flight leave? I still want to catch up on what's been going on in your life and also take you for a bite to eat."

"Randall, that's not necessary."

"Sure it is. I know you're hungry, woman. You have to eat. I heard your stomach growling. And from what I remember, you used to love to eat."

Jada smiled, watching his eyes smile at her. "My flight actually leaves in the morning. I'm going to stay at a hotel tonight."

"No, you're not. You're staying here at my place tonight. I have plenty of guest rooms."

"I couldn't impose."

"You're not imposing. You're staying. Now let's go and get some good grub. There's this great spot called Alexander's. They have Austrian food, Italian food, and lots of seafood. All their food is so good, it'll make your toes wiggle."

To that, they both chuckled.

Chapter Four

Randall wheeled his silver Mercedes Benz away from the villas and cruised down the main road. Often while he drove, he glimpsed aside at Jada. Looking out the window, she enjoyed the island's lush landscapes. He enjoyed the lush sight of her.

He still couldn't believe she actually sat beside him, her skin glowing from the sun's sultry breath, her sensuous eyes sparkling, and those legs so pretty that he had glanced down at them likely a hundred times. Remarkably her waist remained as tiny as it used to be, although she had gained several luscious pounds in the hips that aroused him each time he looked at her. God knows time had blessed her, making her sexier.

He knew she had no idea how much he had thought about her over the years. He always wondered if her life had turned out the way she hoped. He prayed that it did. So many times he had picked up the phone to call her. Other times he picked up a pad and pen to write her letter. But the unexpected that awaited him at Carolyn's bed-side so long ago made him feel guilty. To this day, Kelly didn't even know the full truth. Back then he had no choice but to forsake Jada because of it.

So he longed for Jada secretly and painfully. Years and years after they parted, he could hear a song and it reminded him of her. He could even lay his head on a pillow, close his eyes, and see her face as clear as his own. Fragrances also affected him. Fruity scents always made him feel lustful be-cause she used to rub on those types of body oils and creams. Just the thought of her could make him so rock-hard excited that at times it was nearly unbearable.

Kelly reported that she worked in real estate. More personal information he pried out of his sis-ter. He learned when Jada became engaged to her college sweetheart, when she married him, when they divorced, and now that her fiancé and she had broken their engagement. Kelly never pro-vided details of the breakups, although he begged her to. He was possessed with an unquenchable in-terest in Jada's life.

"So you never opened your bookstore?" he asked.

Jada's lips formed a tremulous smile. "No, never did. Every time I seemed to save enough money or get my credit perfect to get a loan, I needed the money for something else." She thought of the money she squandered on her in-laws, but felt more lighthearted about the family responsibilities she had taken on. No, she didn't have her business. But helping her family meant something. They loved her and that always warmed her heart.

"But you started yours big time," she said, look-

ing at his handsome profile and gazing lower to
his mountain of a chest. She sat up straighter to
temper the feminine twinges she felt. "And if I
haven't said it, I'm so proud that you became this
big real estate tycoon, just like you dreamed."

Randall's enticing lips looked even more so as
he grinned. "Now, I wouldn't call myself a tycoon."

"Kelly does. She called me when you made your
first big purchase of property and she was ecstatic
when your business made it to the *Black Enterprise*
Top 100."

"Oh, I'm just a brother trying to make things
happen," he said as if it were no big deal. "But I really want to thank you for coming on board. I
know it's going to be a big adjustment to be away
from your family. But who knows? Maybe you might
want to send for them. I remember how close you
were to them."

Randall steered his Benz near the front of the
restaurant. While he turned off the ignition, he
noticed Jada's expression. Even though she talked
and seemed pleasant as always, something remained
guarded about her. He sensed what it was. "Jada, I
owe you an explanation."

Jada's heart sped at the mention of rehashing
those old, painful memories. If she had started
talking about it, she feared she would cry and
never stop.

"Randall, you don't owe me anything," she lied.
"The past is the past. Now let's go in and eat. I'm
hungry. I want to eat some of this food that will
make my toes wiggle."

Randall laughed and Jada laughed at herself.
Matter of fact, she laughed more than she wanted
to for the remainder of the day. Randall acted so

kindly and went out of his way to ensure that she had a good time. He made it impossible to hold on to the feeling that hung in the back of her mind about what had occurred long ago.

During their early dinner, they savored scrumptious cuisine. Bacon-wrapped chicken breast had Jada smacking her tongue. Randall polished off his lamb tenderloin with a mint port sauce in seconds and had to order more. Neither could devour enough of the seafood pasta spiced up with shrimp, clams, crab, and other fish delicacies that delighted their palates.

Captivated by a view overlooking the harbor, they chatted about their career paths. They conversed about them so pleasantly that Randall couldn't help taking a journey into the past. "I bought some property in Savannah, and whenever I'm there I visit Ms. Emma."

"I call her occasionally," Jada said and tried to conceal her reluctance to speaking about her dear, elderly friend. Ultimately she knew it would lead to a conversation about their long-ago romance. "I'm so glad that she's doing so well and running her business at this age." She took a sip of her ice-cold virgin daiquiri and set it back down. "Ms. Emma is something else."

"Yes, she is," Randall agreed, picking up a roll. "Do you know that when her doctor told her that she was eating fatty food that was attributing to minor health problems she had, she became a vegetarian? As good a soul food cook as she is, she went to vegetarianism."

Jada laughed softly at Ms. Emma's spunk. "Like I said, she is something."

"Now she is in perfect health and even jogs for

an hour every day. She says that her doctor even has a picture of her in his office. She says he shows it off to his other patients and tells them that this is the most perfect patient he has."

"She told me that she can outrun Gregory," Jada added. "Can you imagine? Your elderly mama runs so fast and is in such good shape that she can outrun you. Gregory should be ashamed."

Randall laughed, his shoulders shaking. "The man doesn't care about running like an Olympian. He is the playboy of Savannah."

A smile tugged at Jada's lips. "It figures. He seemed kind of frisky when we were there."

"Frisky. Shoot, the man is the lover man. Says he is never settling down. His ways, in regard to women, remind me so much of my brother Hunter that it isn't even funny."

Jada was tickled again. "Gregory was nice though."

"Yes, he's a cool guy. Funny, too. Those were some nice times." He nodded, staring at her.

Gazing back at him, Jada felt heat flare in her face. "Ms. Emma had a nice place."

"And the memories," he said, his gaze floating across her features, settling at her lips. "I have such incredible memories."

Nodding, Jada felt the heat descending over her flesh. "Me too."

Randall reached across the table, clutched her hand, and in a lower voice uttered, "You made those memories unforgettable."

Her body tingled from his touch, but her heart ached from wounds of long ago. Jada unhooked her hand from his and asked, "So what is the first project we will tackle with your villas?"

After leaving the restaurant, Randall drove Jada

around the island, acquainting her with the spectacular sites. For some moments, they rode in strained silence. However, for the duration of the ride, they had a pleasurable conversation about her new position, travel, and good things that happened in their families.

They also discovered their mutual love of fixing up homes. Randall expressed that he planned to refurbish a shuttered hotel he owned on the island with a friend. Jada claimed to be an expert at minor renovations and offered her muscle when they started the work. Randall promised to hold her to that when the restoration commenced.

By the time they arrived back at his mansion, it approached midnight. Jada settled into a plush bedroom, but had too many thoughts to sleep. Her emotions were mixed and they overwhelmed her. Of course, getting a job she loved excited her. Complete with an outstanding salary, it also had the advantage of coming with a furnished villa and allowing her to reside on a breathtaking tropical island.

Realistically, though, how could she work with Randall? How could she even consider working with him on a day-to-day basis? Once she saw him on that patio, the entire day had felt surreal. Jada still felt dazed by it all.

And what was wrong with seeing him the way she did and *feeling* the way she did? Time hadn't stolen any of his sex appeal. He was so male and she was so aware of him that her body still felt weakened and turned on in the most intimate places.

It was déjà vu, as if she were a young girl again, captivated by him. What played with her emotions most was the way Randall looked at her. He made her feel beautiful, desirable, as if all he lived for was to be with her. That's how he used to make her feel long ago. But because of his disappearing act, she knew that was a lie. All he wanted was her body. Once it was out of sight, she was out of mind.

Even so, with all the reasons she should have turned down this position, she knew she had too many debts and expenses of her own and her family's to do so. What a mess Kelly had gotten her into. Throughout the day, it took Jada's greatest acting ability not to show how much heartache Randall had caused her. So many times she had laughed with him, when she really wanted to cry, "You just don't know how bad you hurt me."

The most difficult part of the entire situation was just wondering how she could get beyond the feelings she still harbored for him. Whatever desires he had awakened within her had to cease. Randall was her employer now. More than that, he was a man capable of hurting her, just like Michael had, just like Derrick had—just like he had before. Her heart just wasn't up for the agony.

Jada hoped stepping into the shower might make her thoughts of Randall fade and help her sleep. By the time she dried herself of warm droplets and rubbed her mixed-fruit-scented oil all over her body, she no longer thought of what they did during the day, or what they had talked about, or what working with him would be like, or what they meant to each other, or what he had done to her so long ago. Sensual images invaded her mind. Sensual images of Randall and her. They made her feel so sexy that she slipped into a slinky black teddy.

* * *

Clad only in his pajama bottoms, Randall strolled into the kitchen to get his usual late night snack of Lay's Potato Chips and onion dip. He had developed the habit of snacking before bedtime during these past few years. His brothers Hunter and Jackson had claimed that nerves made him crave the bedtime treats.

They claimed that Randall's nerves had been rattled when his ex, Selena, betrayed him in a way that no man could bear. Randall disagreed. He considered the snacks merely comfort food. Besides, each morning he worked the calories off for an hour in his basement gym.

Randall started to reach into the cabinet, but stalled because of his mental dialogue. His mind gave him no peace. The shock of being reunited with Jada hadn't settled in. Her presence in St. Thomas, and in his bedroom, and the fact that he would be working with her, made everything all the more astonishing. The day had been dreamlike. Whether that was good or bad, he didn't know.

What was he thinking when he hired her? He knew the answer to that. He thought with both of his heads.

Jada acted as sweet and warmhearted as she did years ago. He cherished that down-to-earth quality about her. Above anything, it made her sexy.

He recalled how addictive he was to her company when they stayed at Ms. Emma's place. They always had so much to talk about, such as their hopes and dreams, and their families. More beautiful, she always encouraged him to be all he could be. To this day, no other woman encouraged his dreams the way she had.

Jada had made him feel so special. At every chance, he tried to make her feel special, too. Because she was. She was so precious.

When they were together, they existed in this special world of their own. It was filled with love, desire, respect, dreams, and so much more. Only with her could he live in that world, because only the two of them could create it.

But he would have been lying to himself if he had said that only their mental and spiritual connection affected him. Jada was so superfine that when he hugged her, Randall skillfully maneuvered the front of his body in such a way so she couldn't feel the brunt of his excitement.

Simply looking at her stimulated him so much, he knew no other woman could make him feel that way. No other woman had ever given him the degree of male desire that Jada had, and they hadn't even made love.

Making love—it was all Randall thought about during the day with Jada. Making the love that fate had robbed from them. It had been a long time since he wanted to grab a woman and love her until she screamed with satisfaction, and then hold her tenderly in his arms, telling her how much she had meant to him. His ex-fiancée, Selena, had been the only one who had truly touched his soul since Jada. But after what she did, he had been turned off by the opposite sex.

Women then became friends and companions, and some sexual partners. Yet no one had touched him inside—at least not until today. Despite the protective armor Jada wrapped around herself, somehow she made him feel what he had felt long ago with her.

He knew the warmth and openness that lay beneath her shield. He knew how much she could love a man and make him feel loved. Being around her reminded him how much he could feel. But how could he entertain having a romance with her now? Jada was an employee.

Randall scolded himself for not telling her that he needed time to think about hiring her. He had done that with other applicants. But her credentials were the most impressive he had seen of those he interviewed. That shouldn't have surprised him. He knew Jada would do well in life.

He knew she would put her heart into everything she did. He had even been envious over the years, knowing she had put her heart into some lucky guy out there in the world. He ached because that man was not him. Instead of loving her every day of his life, he had been sent on another road to rescue someone.

How he had longed to explain what happened long ago. If only she would let him. From the sadness that hid in her eyes throughout the day, Randall knew what occurred years ago was just as real today in her heart. If given the chance to share his side, he believed it would tear down the wall he felt between them.

Randall intended to go straight to his room when he removed his munchies from the cabinet, but found his bare feet thumping toward Jada's bedroom door. He raised his hand to knock. That's when he happened to notice the door cracked slightly. More than that, he observed Jada sashaying about the room, preparing for bed.

Um, he thought. Was that a little nightgown she wore, or was that some fabric put together specifically for her body to drive a man out of his mind? From her head to her toes, he enjoyed the view. Only an unexpected glance in his direction jolted him from his pleasure.

"Randall, do you want something in here? Come in and get it if you do."

Chapter Five

"No, actually, I wanted to give you something," Randall replied, unable to avert his gaze from her night-wear. His eyes flitted over her so much that he knew it made no sense to cover up what he thought. "That's—that's nice what you're wearing there."

"Thank you."

Jada glanced down at her seductive sleepwear, knowing she should have thrown on her kimono before inviting him inside the bedroom. She gazed back up at Randall and pretended that she was unaware he wore no pajama top. But even when her attention aimed at a respectable place, his face, her mind had already framed that broad chest and those large, muscled arms attached to it. Weakness seized her legs once again.

Randall walked into the room. "I usually have a snack at night. Just wanted to know if you would like something, too."

"No, thank you," Jada said with a quick look at

the chips. "I'm not hungry. Just want to get to bed so I can make my early flight tomorrow. Maybe I can catch a few winks."

"All right then. If you need anything, I'm just down the hall."

Moments later, Jada lay among the darkness in her bed, entangled in the sheets. No matter which way she turned or how cozy she attempted to make herself, sleep evaded her. All the natural wonders on that gorgeous creature down the hall kept her awake. Now how was she going to work with the man if he turned her on like this?

She wasn't even behaving like herself. Why had she flaunted her little teddy when she could have thrown on a cover-up? She knew why. She yearned to feel pretty and seductive, and for Randall to behold her *that way*. She yearned to see that look of hunger on Randall's face and know that she put it there. She yearned to look in his eyes and see that he wanted something only she could give. She certainly saw an eyeful, too. But was it wishful thinking that it was red-hot desire for her?

Down the wide, lengthy hallway inside a master bedroom, Randall lay awake in the dark, too. Images of Jada in that wicked black teddy robbed him of slumber. Closing his eyes, Randall could still visualize Jada's shapely legs, hips, and cleavage. He heard her sensuous voice, smelled the fruity cream slathered on her skin, and ever so slowly touched her. Every inch of her and every crevice, his fingers wandered along and into. So much so, his loins soon played the game of how-hard-can-you-get?

Randall thought about Jada until he perspired

and became restless. He grabbed his robe and decided to walk along the grounds. He loved midnight strolls.

Outside, the moon cast a silvery light over his land and he headed toward his favorite tree. It had a spectacular view of the ocean. But when he neared his destination, a sight stunned him. Jada was relaxing on the ground, her back against his much-loved tree.

Long lashes shadowing her cheeks flew up with her surprise at seeing him. "I hope you don't mind my being here in the middle of the night. It's just that I couldn't sleep."

Randall dropped down on the ground beside her. "Of course I don't mind. I couldn't sleep either."

Jada wondered what had kept him up. "I went for a short walk and then I just found this tree. It looked like it was calling me."

Randall gazed aside at her delicate profile. "I bet you won't believe this."

"What?"

"This is my favorite tree. Out of all of the trees on this estate, I always come here and sit. I love the view of the ocean from here." He inhaled deeply, loving the salt-sprinkled air.

"That is something. Maybe we have some psychic connection going on." She gazed out at the ocean and watched the waves crashing against the shore. Then suddenly she felt Randall watching her. She tightened the sash of her robe and smiled at him. "You live in a beautiful place, Randall."

"I've been blessed . . . in many ways," he said, continuing to stare at her.

Jada's gaze fused with his until those old familiar stirrings prodded her belly. She shifted her attention back to the sea, although she couldn't focus because she knew Randall watched her.

"Do you entertain a lot?" she asked, attempting to lessen the tension she felt. "I bet people love to come here and look out at this view."

"I entertain some. I bet you're going to be entertaining a lot at your place." He had seen how the men stared at her today when they were out. He imagined her having plenty of male companionship; that is, if she didn't have a new boyfriend accompanying her to St. Thomas. "Is anyone coming from home to help you get settled in?"

"No, it's going to be just me," she said with a sigh.

Glumness in her tone brought to mind her broken engagement that Kelly had told him about. "I guess you wanted a new start after everything," he said, hoping he wasn't about to overstep his bounds.

Kelly had always been discreet about sharing others' confidences, so Jada was a bit miffed to hear this. Where else could Randall have heard it from? "And why do you say that?"

"Because I always ask Kelly about you."

"You do?"

"Yes, I do. And she doesn't tell much, but one of the things I managed to get out of her is that you had a broken engagement in January."

Jada took a deep breath. Michael was the last thing she wanted to think about. She guessed he had brought it up because of his own situation. "Kelly usually doesn't tell much, you're right. But she told me about your broken engagement also." She debated asking what happened when suddenly a sharp pain stabbed her in the right buttock.

Randall frowned seeing her frown. "What's the matter?"

"Oh, this is so embarrassing."

"What? What's wrong?"

Jada hopped up. "Something is stuck in my . . ."

Randall glimpsed her hand. She pointed to her backside. "Your butt?"

With a silly grin, Jada shook her head. "I better go in the house."

Randall watched her dash off and then followed her.

Several minutes after she darted into her room, Randall knocked on her door. "Is everything all right in there?"

"Uh . . ."

"Jada, are you okay? You want to go to the doctor?"

Jada opened the door.

Randall's eyes widened, beholding her in the short black teddy again. It was so short that he couldn't wait for her to turn around to see what the back view of it looked like on her. "So you have it out?"

Flustered, Jada shook her head. "I need you to get it out. I mean, if you don't mind."

Randall swallowed and questioned his hearing. "You mean . . . you mean you want me to get it out?" He arched his brows. "From behind?"

Jada sighed with frustration. Her fingers couldn't grasp the wood, splinter, or whatever it was from her buttocks. She couldn't see back there. The mirror hadn't helped. "It's so painful that I can't wait. All you have to do is lift the side of my teddy slightly. And it's at the bottom of my . . . my butt cheek."

Randall swallowed again. When they were in love

years ago, she had driven him crazy by stroking his body and letting her stroke his until they experienced an erotic madness. Still, they had never gotten to the point of seeing each other fully naked. Therefore, he never had the pleasure of viewing her apple-shaped bottom bare.

Just the thought of being up close and personal with that part of her anatomy made his chest heave. With it, his temperature rose so highly he wondered if the air conditioner still worked in the house.

"Sure. I'll do anything to help you," he responded with a clearing of his throat. He walked into the room, feeling uneasy and excited altogether. "I don't want you to be in pain."

Jada also felt awkwardness and embarrassment as she turned her back to Randall. Instantly she became aware of him kneeling down behind her and then suddenly fingertips grazed her sensitive flesh. Gentler than she had ever been touched, he raised the right side of the teddy's fabric and caressed the painful spot on her bottom.

"Yes, that's it," Jada said, feeling a pleasing sensitivity that spread to her feminine core.

Inspecting the area, Randall nodded. "I see it."

His heart raced wildly. Sweat droplets dotted his forehead. But his fingers remained steady when he grasped the tiny piece of wood from the smoothest, roundest, prettiest bottom he had ever seen, although his lips trembled as his face closed in on the wood. After all, Jada was in pain.

"If I hurt you, let me know."

"Go ahead. Do it."

Randall proceeded with the most pleasurable task he had had in a long time. As he tugged the wood, he inhaled fruity oils and knew that Jada rubbed it everywhere and not solely on her legs. Firmness hit sharp between his legs and he began to crave the taste of fruit oils and the feeling of much more.

"Are you almost there? Is it coming?"

Something was coming, all right, Randall thought. But he had to get a grip on his extreme attraction to Jada. The woman was in pain. With this in mind, he refocused.

"I have it," he said, standing, and then tossed the tiny piece of wood in the container. "You better go put some alcohol on that, so it won't get infected." He wanted to offer to do it for her, but she might have thought he was fresh.

Jada smiled shyly. "Thank you, Randall. This was *sooooo* embarrassing."

"No, it could happen to anyone. It's my fault. I have to check around that tree. We don't want it to happen to you again."

Jada wondered if that meant he would be inviting her over to his place frequently. She also wondered why his hands had felt so tantalizing on her bare backside.

Minutes later, she sprawled in bed, mentally recreating the earlier moments. Odd as it was, even though her rear end had hurt, the way Randall removed the splinter hadn't smarted at all. In fact, she wouldn't have minded getting another back there for him to take out.

Down the hall, Randall knew he wouldn't be able to sleep. A cold shower beckoned him. He hopped in it, turning it on full blast.

"What have I gotten myself into?" he thought aloud.

Chapter Six

The morning Jada returned from her Fourth of July celebration with her family, she settled into her villa. Decorated in mostly beige and white, it had ultramodern furnishings, appliances, and architecture. Jada felt pampered in every room.

After her flight from New Jersey, she yearned to freshen up with a shower. Inside the bathroom, she marveled at the lavishness she basked in. Courtesy of Randall, she had the softest green marble floor, sink, cabinets, and Jacuzzi.

Once her clothes were shed, she closed her eyes and let the warm stream cascade over her limbs. With every sliver that slid over her skin, she imagined Randall's fingertips exploring her body, setting it aflame. While he removed that splinter, it took all of her strength for her not to expose more of her body for his delicate, but extremely manly handling.

During the Fourth of July barbecue feast with her family, her body was present; her mind was far away. Randall was all she thought about; Randall touching her in such an intimate place; Randall staring in her eyes as if he was sending her a secret message "I want you"; Randall talking to her as if their past meant as much to him as it did to her. Most of all, she sat dazed thinking that Randall was in her life again. It still hadn't sunk in.

That all being as it was, she knew her obsession with him had to stop. She had to keep reminding herself that Randall was her boss. More importantly, Randall was the man who shattered her heart.

Once Jada had showered and massaged her favorite body lotion on her legs, arms, and chest, she wiggled into a sleeveless, pastel peach dress and slipped her feet into high-heeled mules of the identical color. To top off the look, she wore gold hoop earrings and pulled her hair back in a loose ponytail. Plagued with butterflies in her stomach, she strolled across the courtyard to the management office.

Randall opened the door for a stout, freckled, senior gentleman to leave just as Jada arrived on his doorstep. Being in Randall's presence once again filled her with emotions that she wished she didn't feel.

Randall divided a beguiling smile between Jada and the man exiting his office. "Gus, this is Jada, my property manager. We've known each other a long time." He granted her an affectionate look. "She's new to St. Thomas. And, Jada, this is Gus. He's a longtime friend and mentor, and he owns that old hotel with me that I was telling you about."

"Welcome to the island, dear," Gus said with a grin that made two shiny balls of his cheeks. "You're going to enjoy it here. And, Randall, you watch yourself, son, you might not be able to concentrate with such a beautiful woman working with you."

Jada blushed. "It's very nice meeting you, Gus."

"We'll be seeing each other often, dear. This young man is like a son to me." He patted Randall's shoulder and drove off in a small red truck.

Gus left them in a lighthearted mood. Jada and Randall made small talk about their holidays; that is, until Jada stated her eagerness to get started at her job.

Randall moved aside to let Jada enter the office. Her sexy, sweetish scent caressed his senses. Keenly his eyes trailed her movements as she checked out the place. Her round buttocks had the careful, seductive rhythm of a slow-walking cat and reminded Randall that a luscious set of back pockets was his favorite sight blessed from nature.

It had been his pleasure to handle one of her back pockets the other night. Each time he thought about the incident, he smiled. Even during an important meeting earlier in the day, he thought about their doctor-patient moment. He smiled so much that the others at the conference begged him to share what amused him so much. He replied, "Sorry, it's my little secret."

Jada's hips' sensuous sway lured Randall down to her legs. Her peach minidress and the matching shoes flaunted them well. Bare, oiled, and shapely, her calves, thighs, and ankles instantly beckoned to his mind delightful fantasies, although when Jada spun around, his gaze was directed at her face.

She noticed that they were the only people in the four offices. "Where is everyone?"

"You're the first one I've hired, so that means once you and I get settled you're going to have to help me hire some folks."

She granted him a sensuous smile. "Whatever you want, boss. Now I think it's about time I get acquainted with my work. So, can you show me to my office and my duties?"

Disappointment dulled the upbeat expression Randall had since he last saw her. In just that short time away from her, he had missed her. Nonetheless, here she was again in business mode. He didn't know what he had expected on her return, but it seemed they should have been talking more and been less impersonal. He had to remind himself that they were employer and employee.

"Okay, let's get to it," he said.

Much of the afternoon, Randall familiarized Jada with her responsibilities. Most of it consisted of paperwork concerning the tenants that he had already rented to. The other part dealt with details about the vacant villas that he hoped to rent in the coming weeks. Randall found Jada to be a hard worker and a sharp one.

Even so, with each moment spent around her, he felt tension. Sometimes he believed it was sexual tension. Then he would question if that was wishful thinking. Other times, he sensed tension of another kind.

"Jada," he said, shuffling into her office, his hands stuck in his pockets, "is something bothering you?"

She laughed as if he sounded ridiculous. "What

could be bothering me? I'm living on a beautiful island and I've just started a great job."

"Don't you think it's time we had that talk?"

"What talk?"

"About us ... the past ... what happened. The reason I ..."

Immediately Jada turned on her computer and directed her interest to it. "Randall, that was so long ago. I really don't think about it that much and neither should you. Who needs to get hung up on that old stuff? I better get to this."

Randall nodded and stood in the room a moment, watching her. At one point, she looked up at him and a smile radiated from her lips. But her eyes reflected something else—something else that bothered him.

Early in the evening, they decided to wrap up their workday. Randall invited Jada for a stroll behind the villas. He bragged about a cluster of palm trees that formed a path.

"I'm not up to a walk," she said. "I need to go home and do some more unpacking."

"Aw, come on," he insisted. "I need you to see it back here, so you can describe it to potential tenants who call or give them a tour when they drop by."

With that pitch, Jada couldn't deny him. She let him lead the way.

The grassy backland of the villas immersed Jada in a tropical garden that took her breath away. A myriad of palm trees stood in rows shading the scenery, allowing a limestone pathway between them. Multihued fish swam in two small ponds. A small statue of a bronzed African warrior poured water into a fountain.

Bright red, yellow, and orange orchids, poinsettias, and philodendrons blossomed in flower beds. Their bouquet perfumed the surroundings with a scent that was both citruslike and sweet. Complete with the Caribbean Sea glistening in the distance, a stroll was pure splendor.

"Yes, this is something to see," Jada said, stepping beside Randall, admiring the beauty. "It is best that I see it to describe it. I'm going to write up a brochure about this, too."

"Great. I hoped you would do that. That's why I wanted you to see it and experience it."

"In fact," she elaborated, "if I go home now, I can get a start on that while my mind is fresh with these images. I can unpack later."

Randall took a long-winded breath. "Do you want to get away from me that bad?"

"No, of course I don't want to get away from you." Nervously Jada chuckled.

"Then why are you trying to cut short our being together? And why are you holding back from me?"

She froze, making his steps cease, too. "Randall, what are you talking about?"

"I'm talking about us, Jada. There is this tension between us." Gently his gaze searched her face. "And I know it's because of what happened. I know it's because I chose Carolyn over you."

Silence suddenly hung between them, filled only by birds chirping. Jada's throat tightened. It strangled any intelligible word she intended to speak. Promptly she turned away from him, so he wouldn't see the tears that fought to escape from her. But still *I chose Carolyn over you* rang in her head and smothered her heart. When Randall clutched her arms, easing her around to face him, she put forth her greatest effort not to shed a tear.

"What do you want me to say, Randall? You want me to talk about how it felt receiving one call and one letter from you, after all we had meant to each other? You want me to tell you how I jumped every time the phone rang, praying it was you on the other end ready to tell me how much you loved me? You want me to say how much I rummaged through the mail every day, hoping to God that you wrote me? You want me to say that every time I came home from school, I prayed that you would be sitting in Ms. Emma's house waiting for me?

"You want me to say that I could have sworn I saw you walking on the campus, and then I got closer to the guy and it wasn't you? You want me to tell you how many songs on the radio reminded me of you, or how many times I thought of you, or how much I cried when I realized you were going to stay with Carolyn? Well, there it is, Randall. You broke my heart, if that's what you want to know." Bubbles of water started blurring her sight, but she was too emotional to care if he saw them now. "I loved you more than I ever loved any man. I still haven't felt that kind of love, not with any of the men I have known over the years, not with my husband, not with my fiancé, not with anyone.

"You were the only one I ever even talked to about my father and what his desertion meant to me. You were the only one who gave me this feeling—*this indescribable feeling* that I can't find anywhere else, *anywhere*. I still can't understand how one summer with someone can make you feel closer to them than you have felt with anyone else. I've been with guys for years; I was married; I've had a fiancé; and still that time with you is *so* unforgettable.

"I can't understand it. I wish I could, but I can't. So now you know. You know how much you hurt me. It's all out now. And I do forgive you. So now let's just get on with our working relationship and leave it behind."

"I'm so sorry that the pain is all so fresh for you," he said, brushing her tears away with his fingertips. "But if it's any consolation, I hurt, too, Jada. I'm sorry I sent you only one letter and called only once. But you have no idea what waited for me when I returned home. First, there was Carolyn in that intensive care unit. She was all messed up, near death with all types of injuries. When I had the chance, I called you. And then I wrote you, too. I wanted to be with you so bad, but I knew she needed me there. So I thought, I'd hold her hand for a while to help her get better and then I would return to you."

"But you didn't return to me. There was just that one call and one letter and you forgot all about me."

"No, you're wrong. You were always with me in my mind and heart. But I learned something that changed so much. Not only had Carolyn almost gotten killed in the car accident, but she had nearly killed a baby she carried—*my* baby."

Chapter Seven

Jada gasped. "What? She was pregnant?" Her hand flew up to her chest. "Oh my God."

"She was three months. We had to have conceived our baby our last time together. But I didn't know she was pregnant."

Jada's head spun with this news. "I didn't know that. Kelly didn't tell me. Kelly has never told me you had a child with Carolyn."

"Kelly didn't know. She still doesn't. The only people that have ever known were Carolyn and I, our parents, two of my brothers, Hunter and Jackson, and my friend Gus. Our child . . . our child didn't live. Carolyn lost him during her lengthy hospital stay. She and the baby had been too badly injured."

"I don't know what to say." She shook her head, trying to absorb this news. "I'm—I'm sorry you lost your child. I wouldn't wish that on anyone, Randall."

"When we broke up, she found out she was carrying my child. But she said that she didn't want to hold on to me that way. When she lost the baby at the hospital, she was so torn up. So was I.

"It was so hard then. I wanted to be with you. God knows I wanted to be with you, but it was wrong to just leave her and return to you, when she was so sick and had just lost our baby. I told my parents how much I loved you and wanted to be with you.

"But you have to understand, Jada, what kind of family I come from. They are good people. *Good* people. But they kept telling me that it would be wrong to abandon Carolyn and be with you.

"They kept telling me how much Carolyn needed me, and that it was wrong to just run off and go on about my life after she had lost my child. And I knew I wasn't raised that way. I couldn't just abandon her after what she had gone through. What kind of man does something like that?

"I felt so guilty about what I felt for you. I felt so guilty that I thought it would be best not to call you for a while or write. Something seemed wrong about it every time I looked at poor Carolyn fighting for her life or crying about our baby that she lost. Then something miraculous happened. Carolyn started getting better. Everyone said it was because of me. I don't know. I just think it was God's will.

"Whatever the reason, she became well enough to recuperate at home. So I stuck by her then, too. And that's when she started to depend on me. She started to believe that we were meant to be back together and that I loved her as much as she loved me. It was such a difficult time, because . . . because all I could think about was you."

Pausing, he stared at Jada silently. "From the

time I woke in the morning until my head hit the pillow, I thought of you. Every time Carolyn hugged me or kissed me, or even . . . loved me, I thought of you. God knows I felt horrible about being with one woman and thinking about another. I kept telling myself that I had to get you out of my head and my heart.

"But you never went away. I know better than anyone that you can't make yourself stop feeling and wanting someone. You can't make yourself stop thinking about them, no matter how wrong you know it is.

"You were always with me. Even over the years. I understand what you mean when you talk about spending one summer with someone and they make you feel like no one else ever has. You go through your life and you can be with people for months and years, and what you feel with them never comes close to what you felt with that one special person in that short period of time." He stepped closer to her, inhaling her succulent scent. "Please forgive me for not standing up and being a man. I should have gone back to Savannah to love you the way you deserved to be loved."

His nearness ignited a potent awareness of him. "It's a comfort to know that you were being a decent man and sticking by a woman that had carried your child. But it still hurts, Randall."

"I know. There are no words that can express how sorry I am that I hurt you. I've had so many regrets over the years about what I did to us." He studied her as she looked off in the distance, and asked, "So where do we go from here?"

Jada wiped her eyes and tried not to get lost in

his compelling stare. "I don't want to be hurt again. I'm just so tired of it. My fiancé and I were going to be married this month. I'm so tired of the seesaw of love. I'm so tired of having my hopes and all my love thrown back in my face. I—I want to be alone. I just want to love myself right now."

"I know how you feel, Jada. Ever since I broke up with my fiancée, I have stayed clear of relationships. The misery she gave me brought me so down. Even when I was around people laughing and talking, in the back of my mind I had this weight on my heart. I couldn't shake it off either.

"And I've been with women since then, but it was understood on both sides that it was nothing serious. We were in a sense just sex partners. And that's because I couldn't feel anything. I was that torn up about what happened with my fiancée. But since I've been reunited with you again, I would like to change that." He eased his hands onto her shoulders, relishing the feel of her soft skin again. "I would like to get to know you again and see where it could lead us."

"I would like to get to know you, too, Randall," she agreed, loving his strong hands holding her. "But my heart has been broken too much for . . . And even though I understand how you couldn't abandon an injured woman who lost your child, in the end you chose to be with Carolyn. You resumed your relationship with her even when she was well. And you never contacted me again. You never even said good-bye."

"That's because by the time I realized it was hurting both Carolyn and myself to pretend I wanted to be with her, it was too late to be with you again." He caressed her shoulders, aching to caress all over her, and his voice dipped low with his growing desire. "Kelly told me you were engaged."

"Why shouldn't I have been engaged?" she asked, fighting the sensations his every stroke stirred within her. "Not hearing from you was horrible. It was the worst thing that ever happened to me. I questioned everything you ever said to me. I felt so empty inside. It was like a toothache that I carried around with me every day. That sadness never went away. I can't risk that happening again; I can't even try."

"It won't happen again."

"Those are your words, Randall. Your actions long ago spoke the truth."

"So you're saying that after everything we meant to each other, we're just going to wind up being friends?" He dropped his hands to her waist, drawing their bodies close.

Jada inhaled sharply from the sudden impact of his hard body against hers. Womanly hunger spread down from her chest, throbbing between her thighs. Her heart racing, she divulged in a near whisper, "Friendship is all I can offer."

Randall's gaze slowly dragged across her sensuous features. As he tightened his hold of her, his manhood turned to stone a thousand times over, and he could tell from the look on her face that she felt every inch of his excitement. "There is something I want to get out of my system before we get on with our friendship," he whispered. "If we deal with it now, we'll never have to bother with it again."

"What's that?" she asked breathlessly.

"This," Randall said, bending his head to her face.

His mouth moved over hers slowly, granting her what she had long starved for. Her body quivered as her lips parted. His tongue set out to explore. Once he was all the way in, he unlocked a pleasure chest.

Sensations that she hadn't felt in twenty years, and sensations that she had never felt, set a fire in her blood. To be kissed so passionately by Randall again felt so good that Jada could not help lacing her arms around his shoulders. She had no choice but to moan, letting him know she craved more.

She couldn't feel enough of his solid body molding to the feminine contours of hers. She couldn't inhale enough of his masculine cologne sprinkled at his collarbone. She couldn't get enough of his tongue slinking around hers so erotically that each swerve of it affected her as if he kissed between her legs. Over and over a painfully sweet fullness grew in the base of her stomach. Over and over it burst, drenching her panties.

The hardness she felt prodding deep into her clothed flesh intensified the taste of his kiss. Helpless, Jada was, as his love writhed against her. The deeper their mouths mated in their titillating dance, the more Jada trembled with an insatiable need to be one with him.

So caught up in the ecstasy was Randall that he maneuvered his tongue with the in-and-out motions that were reminiscent of intercourse. He couldn't get enough of tasting her. He couldn't quell his extreme desire to bury himself within her honeyed walls and feel what he had never had. He knew she

had to feel like heaven. He had dreamed it endlessly. It all made him groan his hot need into their
entwined mouths.

Her whimpers of rapture thrilled him and hardened him another rung. How he had missed kissing her. How he had missed holding her warm
flesh, smelling her fruity fragrance, hearing her
sexy voice, beholding her seductive walk, talking
to her, and never wanting it to end. How he had
missed everything about Jada. No other woman
could make him feel the way she did.

Greedily he kissed her. All the while, he steered
her back toward a tree. As he pinned her back
against it, Randall pushed himself against her
deeper. He kissed her deeper. Her sweetness
caused him to tremble and his stomach to clench.
He ached to be inside her. He ached to taste her—
taste every inch of her.

As his chest rose and fell with his quickening
breaths, he sought more of the sugar that set him
afire. While he did so, his hands traced the dra-
matic curves of her body. Along the sides of her
tiny waist, his big hands glided. Along the curves
of her hips, they lingered. Along the top of her
chest, he played a teasing game with his fingers.

Then he kissed the top of her breast. Dipping
his face a bit lower into her blouse, he grew bolder.
He sought out the marble-hard nipples that poked
through her shirt.

"Wait," she said, trying to catch her breath. Realizing that someone might see them, she scoured the
area. "Randall, we have to stop this."

"Why?"

"You know why."

"Because it felt too good?"

She swiped across her perspired brow. "Because someone could see us. And because . . ."

"Because what?"

"Because we're not taking our relationship in this direction."

"Oh, that's right," he said with a sigh. "We can only be friends."

"Yes, that's how it's going to be."

"All right. If that's what you want."

"That is what I want."

"Then friends we'll be," he said, raising his chest. "Because we know there's nothing there anymore anyway, right?" He stared in her eyes.

Jada felt weakened by his gaze and turned away. She still could barely catch her breath.

"There's nothing there, right?" he asked again.

"Right," she mumbled and staggered away from the tree.

Viewing her zigzagging gait, he reached for her arm. "Whoa, you're all right? You feel all right?"

Jada straightened her posture and removed his hand. "I'm fine and I'm going home." She marched away toward the courtyard.

Motionless, Randall stood watching her and smiled with a thought: *We'll be friends all right.*

Chapter Eight

The following day Jada behaved as if nothing had occurred between Randall and her. She pretended that she had not had a sleepless night because of the constant replays of that kiss in her mind, along with the fantasies of so much more that she wanted to do with him.

She attempted to disregard the scent of his cologne when he passed her direction. She tried to forget the feel of him pressed tight to her whenever he strode nearby and she glimpsed his body. She acted as if his voice's rich, masculine timbre had no effect on her, or his rugged swagger, or the suave, intelligent way he conducted his business.

Jada even tried to overlook what a gentleman Randall was. He ordered in a buffet of assorted food for their breakfast and lunch. As well, desserts flown in from his father's gourmet dessert company made mouthwatering snacks.

Randall made sure the air conditioner was turned up to the perfect temperature for her. Bowls of her fruit-scented potpourri scattered about the office space because he knew she adored fruity fragrances. If all that wasn't enough, Randall asked the names of her favorite songs and artists. Forty minutes later, he brought back a collection of smooth R&B and jazz for her to listen to while she worked. To top that off, romance and suspense novels with exciting blurbs were delivered from the local bookstore. Randall had ordered them for her.

Countless times throughout the hours of working with him her emotions clashed. On one hand, she ached to get to know him much better and explore the undeniable chemistry they shared. On the other hand, men had hurt her time and time again. This last time with Michael still felt fresh. What's more, the memories of the hurt Randall inflicted had become renewed.

She couldn't subject herself to all that right now. She couldn't let a man break her spirit so severely that she wound up like her sister, Katherine. She had been wounded so deeply that it had nearly destroyed her mind. It always amazed her that Katherine's husband hadn't hurt her physically, but what he had done to her mentally amounted to bashing her skull. Love was so powerful it scared her sometimes.

Inside his office, Randall shuffled papers, struggling to concentrate on his work. Today had been highly successful and he credited it all to Jada's talent. She had inspected some of the villas for safety, as well as for maintenance and equipment needs. She had solicited a bid for a contractual service and designed a financial spreadsheet for some of the properties' transactions. She had given a prospective tenant a tour of the villas, verified his references, and processed his paperwork.

She had also been a tremendous help when Randall interviewed a groundskeeper for employment that his friend Gus had referred. Unmistakably, Randall knew he had hired the right woman. But undeniably, he didn't just want to be Jada's boss and friend. He wanted to be her lover.

Amid this productive day of working with her, during every second he felt sexual tension between them that wouldn't go away. That kiss hung on the edge of his mind no matter what he did today. It had started teasing him last night after he returned home from being with her, and it never stopped.

Again and again, his mind recreated the taste of her, the feel of her, the smell of her, and the seductiveness of her whimper. Repeatedly he closed his eyes, kissing her again in his mind, and doing much more that made her moan from ecstasy.

The kiss lingering in his mind had been complicated with other things during the day with her. Every time he leaned down over her shoulder to explain something to her, her sweet scent stroked his desire. Every moment that their eyes met, he felt that they were whispering to him, declaring how much she wanted him.

Each time she spoke to him, her voice oozed with sexiness and his name sounded like he heard it for the first time. Each time he watched her shapely body sashay across the room, he became that much more infatuated with her. It all made him remember his hands feeling the contours of her hips and waist, and even the bare breasts that he had touched and kissed so long ago.

Everything she did, and everything she was, possessed him so that often during the day, his rigid maleness made him want to rush into her office, grab her, throw her on the desk, and give her what he had wanted to give her for twenty years.

But that's not what she wanted, so she had said with her mouth. Yet her body's response to him and the magnetism he sensed between them told him otherwise. She sent him mixed messages. Then again, how could he possibly understand the depths of a woman's hurt when man after man had hurt her? Jada was supposed to be a bride this month.

He didn't even understand himself since Jada's return to his life. Days prior to her arrival, getting to know a woman didn't interest him, along with opening up to the possibility of a relationship. The grief Selena had caused him kept his defenses up. Now here he was geared up to take a chance and filled with a wealth of emotions for Jada that almost scared him.

Near the end of the workday, Jada prepared to wrap up her exhilarating first day. She turned off her computer and tidied up her desk. When a thirty-something woman clad in a too-tight, too-short red minidress sashayed into the management office, Jada motioned for her to step farther inside.

"May I help you, miss?"

"I'd like to see that handsome-behind Randall, if he's in," she informed Jada.

Jada took special note of her spicy reference to Randall and then started to buzz his office. Her finger hadn't even pressed the intercom when he stepped out of the door.

"Hey there," the woman gushed, strutting toward Randall with an exaggerated sway of her hips. She stepped so close to him their bodies nearly brushed. "You're looking hot today, Mr. Landlord. Have some time for your favorite tenant? I've been living here two weeks now and you haven't been over to my place yet. What about coming over this evening around 8:00? I'm making my mama's shrimp scampi recipe. I landed two husbands with that recipe, along with a little something else." She winked at Randall.

Jada threw her eyes heavenward.

"You know what, Cindy?" Randall said with laughter coating his words. "I have some things to take care of here, but I may take you up on that. I'll call you as soon as I finish and let you know. I have your number in my files."

"I'm looking forward to it, Mr. Landlord. Did I tell you that I took a class in massage?"

A smile played at the corners of Randall's lips. "Uh, no, you didn't."

"You know now then. If you come over this evening, your body will learn that I was an A student."

Bidding Randall good-bye with another wink, Cindy pranced out of the management office. Approximately ten minutes had passed when Jada knocked on his door.

"Come in," he invited her.

She walked in with her arms crossed. "So you have a dinner invitation."

"Who could turn down shrimp scampi?" He turned away from her to tuck files in a cabinet.

"Are you *really* going to go to her place?"

With his back still facing her, Randall grinned at her curiosity. "Why wouldn't I? She's a nice lady."

"She seems okay. She's a little flashy. *And* she's a tenant. Are you going to start getting involved with tenants personally? I mean, it could lead to some trouble. Besides, she doesn't seem like your type."

Randall swung around, unable to hide how much this entertained him. "What is my type?"

Jada shrugged her shoulders. "I don't know. I've just started being around you again."

"True. But why do you care?"

"I just don't want to see you get yourself in a mess."

"Are you jealous?"

That made her chuckle. "Why would I be jealous?"

"True, too. Why would you? Because when we kissed yesterday, there was nothing there. It was just like . . . just like . . . just like kissing a piece of ham."

Her mouth flopped open.

Randall cleared his throat to restrain from laughing at her face. "We didn't feel anything, right?"

Jada rolled her eyes at him. "Right," she said with a flounce out of the room. "I'll see you tomorrow."

"I'll see you, too," he yelled to her. "But I may come in a little late depending on my night."

To that, he heard the front door slam.

Tickled and flattered at Jada's behavior, Randall searched his tenant files. He located Cindy's number and called her to decline the invitation. He had no intention of accepting anyway. It had all been for show for Jada's benefit. Not only did he shun getting involved with his tenants, but since Jada's emergence back in his life, hers was the only face he longed to gaze upon across a dinner table.

Moments later, Randall sat on the bar stool of a local hangout, the Shalvern Grill. Waiting at the bar for his burger and fries take-out order, he felt silly about making Jada jealous. But at least it assured him when they kissed that he *had* gotten under her skin.

Rowdy laughter intruded on his thoughts. Randall twisted around on his stool to see who disrupted the subdued chatter of patrons and the faint tinkling of notes from a baby grand piano. Amid the amber lighting, his gaze skipped over numerous round cherry-wood tables decked with orange oil candles. His search ended at a rear table in a shadowy corner. An ex-friend had made the ruckus with three other men.

Randall leered at Lincoln McGregor until his ex-buddy spotted him. Immediately Randall swung around, hoping they brought his order soon. The grill's ambiance had suddenly lost its appeal.

"How are you doing, man?" a familiar voice asked.

Chapter Nine

Randall looked aside and squinted, taking a long, good look at Linc. He had not seen him since the night his old friend ripped his life apart. Fortunate for Linc, his brothers Hunter, Jackson, Tyler, and Dustin visited his home during the harrowing occasion. They made great efforts to spare Linc a brutal beating. They also prevented Randall from crossing paths with Linc again in Lakeside, Virginia. They feared Randall might slaughter the man.

"You know I have nothing to say to you," Randall said and eyed the bartender with annoyance for not having his food ready earlier.

Linc adjusted his long legs beneath the stool and his dimples flashed with his awkward smile. "It's been a while, man. Now you're saying we're not even going to act civil to each other. I wish I could do things over. A thousand times I wished I could take it all back. She and I are not even together anymore. We came to the island last fall and we broke up a few months later."

Randall motioned to the bartender with his finger. "Is my order ready?"

The dreadlocked man acknowledged his question with a nod and disappeared behind two swinging doors.

"You and I were like brothers," Linc pointed out. "You *were* the brother I never had. When Gus told me you were on the island, I wanted to come by and see you. I wanted to get things back to where they were. And I want to get our hotel off the ground."

Randall narrowed his eyes at him. "Things will never get back to where they were between us. Are you crazy? Or do you think I am? And as far as business goes, I want nothing to do with you. You don't want to work. You want to party all the time."

"You're wrong, Randall. I don't want to party all the time. I'm just not a workaholic like you. I believe there is a time to work and there is a time to live and enjoy yourself. Anyway, I didn't come over here to get into it with you about that. I want to get things going with the hotel. The Sea Breeze Inn is just sitting there. You're stalling things because of this grudge you have against me. But it's not fair to Gus and me. It's our property, too. Do you remember how excited we were when we flew down here and saw that property? It was like we discovered a diamond mine. Do you remember the three of us getting drunk at that restaurant, celebrating when we closed that deal?"

"That was before I knew how low down you could be," Randall declared with a tightened jaw. "I can't do business with you now. No way in hell."

Linc sighed. "Man, I can understand you not wanting to be my business partner when our *situation* first happened. But time is moving on, Randall. And like I said, she and I are not together anymore. It's time to forget all that and get our business off the ground. That inn's a damn good business investment. I want to rebuild it with you and Gus. I want to get it operational and making money. Stop holding that up, man."

Frowning at Linc, Randall leaned back in his chair. "Like I said, I'm not doing business with you. As far as I'm concerned, only Gus and I own that hotel."

A burst of laughter from Linc's table companions drew Randall's attention in their direction. He noticed that others also gawked at the three men for disturbing the sophisticated atmosphere of the grill. "I see you still hang out with the wrong kind of people," Randall told Linc. "You are judged by the company you keep."

Linc shot him an *oh, please* look. "Look, I didn't come over here for a lecture. I came over here to apologize and to let you know I want to work with you. More than that, I want us to be friends again. Gus wants us to be friends again. You're the only one stopping that."

The bartender handed Randall a hot bag. Its vapors cast a fried-food aroma over the bar counter. Randall thanked the guy and stepped down from the stool. Walking away from Linc, he threw over his shoulder, "Don't get in my face again. Don't even come near me."

Outside in his car, Randall drove out of the parking lot. Heavy traffic stalled him from going as fast as he wanted to. He longed to get home, take off his suit, and chow down. Honking his horn in vain, he stopped as his parley with Linc took over his mind. Dazedly he inclined against his velvety seat cushions, whisked back to a time long ago.

Shortly after his breakup with Carolyn, he had intended to purchase his first piece of real estate. Discovering he didn't have enough savings, he pursued and landed a job with Hillford Development. Gus Hillford, a self-made multimillionaire, ran the company. He owned forty properties.

Randall learned so much from Gus, the greatest lesson being to deal with people in business, and otherwise, with integrity. Often Randall went fishing and golfing with Gus after work hours. Lincoln McGregor, another one of Gus's protégés at the development corporation, always joined them.

"Linc," as he was known to friends and family, became one of Randall's best friends. They had more than most people did in common. Linc's dad made his wealth in the men's clothing industry. Randall's father built his fortune with gourmet desserts. However, neither man wanted to rest on his father's achievement. They set out to seek their own riches in real estate.

After learning as much as they could from Gus, saving investment funds, establishing great credit, and securing sizable loans, Randall and Linc went off on their own with Gus's blessings. Both became highly successful real estate entrepreneurs, buying properties in Virginia and outside of it.

Once they heard about the fantastic real estate opportunities in St. Thomas, Gus, Randall, and Linc flew to the island to scout out land and properties. All three wound up buying land for homes they wanted to build for their personal use. In addition, Randall bought land for luxury villas to rent and Linc purchased a boat for pleasure.

Then together the three men bought an old, deserted hotel called the Sea Breeze Inn. They planned to renovate it and make a fortune. At least they did before Linc's and Randall's personal lives unraveled their shared dream.

Randall had always admired Linc's work ethic. It just didn't compare with his. Whereas Randall worked on weekends and endless hours during the week, Linc cut his workday off at Friday afternoons. Plugging away on a project on the weekend wasn't even considered. Frequently he told Randall he worked too much.

Randall accepted their differences regarding work. After all, they couldn't agree on everything. So when Friday nights came, Linc hung out with his boys, drinking and chasing women. Sometimes his buddies got him in trouble, such as tickets for speeding and home visits from the police for disturbing the peace. Meanwhile, Randall worked tireless hours doing anything from paperwork to making repairs on his properties.

When he met Selena Mason, a makeup artist at Lakeside's local department store, Randall was smitten. She assisted him with purchasing a gift basket for his sister Jessica's birthday present. Selena appeared sexy, nice, smart, and she knew how to make him feel good after a long day of dealing with the real estate business.

After a year and a half of dating, Randall proposed. Selena moved into his Lakeside home and resigned from her position at the department store. Linc threw them the biggest engagement party that their small town had ever seen.

Randall wanted to give her everything. Tirelessly he worked, traveling back and forth from St. Thomas, building Selena and him a mansion on the property he had purchased on the island. He also started construction on his villas and handled details of rebuilding the Sea Breeze Inn. More wonderful, he had a big surprise for Selena.

Yet she never had the satisfaction of basking in what Randall did for her. Continuously she complained about his working too much and traveling too much. She ranted that they never went out anymore or did anything that they did prior to their engagement. Eventually she accused him of having an affair. Randall assured her of his faithfulness. He promised that his extensive work hours resulted from him trying to give her her every heart's desire. He asked her to trust him and be patient.

Then came the night he returned from St. Thomas three days earlier than Selena expected him. His brothers had picked him up from the airport and taken him home, so they could all watch the basketball game together. Randall told them to make themselves comfortable. He encouraged them to raid the refrigerator and cabinets for their game-time snacks.

Meanwhile, he walked upstairs to surprise Selena with his early arrival home. What's more, he wanted to surprise her with the paperwork for the mansion he had built for them on the island. If that weren't enough, he wanted to surprise her with a mansion that he built not far from theirs, for her mother. Selena had always expressed that she would miss her mother if she moved so far away to the tropical paradise.

Walking down the hall to his bedroom, Randall

smiled as he imagined seeing Selena's beautiful face again. He had missed her so much. But suddenly the smile transformed to a frown and Randall froze in his footsteps.

Moans had stunned him so much that he couldn't move. He swore he heard moans coming from his bedroom. Shower water was rushing, so identifying or hearing the sound again became difficult. Still, he listened for it while paralyzed with shock. It took several seconds before he heard it again. Moans had come from his bedroom. Then the sound stopped as soon as it started.

Randall's heart began to beat so fast and powerfully, it felt as if it jerked his entire body. His jaw tightened and he swallowed continuously from the adrenaline juices rushing up in his throat. Stepping toward his bedroom, he listened for the moans again. He heard nothing except the shower's downpour.

Swallowing again, he treaded into the bedroom. His satin sheets were tousled. Traces of perspiration permeated the air. Fierce pounding in Randall's heart intensified and mushroomed. Every part of his body developed its own drumbeat. Randall could not believe what he beheld. Yet he had no choice when he moved farther into the room and looked to Selena's side of the bed. Her clothes and a man's were scattered on the floor.

Moans that sounded near painful startled him. They were louder now because he stood closer to the bathroom and shower. Feeling as if he were someone else, feeling as if this moment were a dream he ached to wake from, Randall trudged to the bathroom. The door stood open. The shower curtain was gathered to one side.

Against the wall, Linc's and Selena's naked bodies locked and moved together.

So intoxicated with passion that their eyes were sealed tight, neither Selena nor Linc saw him.

"I cannot believe what I'm seeing," Randall said with an eerie calmness.

Linc's and Selena's eyes flung open at the sound of his voice.

"I'm sorry, man," Linc apologized, his bright eyes widened, his breaths escaping him. "I didn't mean for this to happen." He gulped. "You know how I feel about you. You're like my brother. She kept throwing it at me and throwing it at me. She—"

"I *did* mean for it to happen!" Selena admitted, tugging wet auburn hair away from her face. "You've been cheating on me! I know it. That's why you never want me to go with you to St. Thomas. I don't believe that nonsense about you working all the time over there and you wouldn't be able to see me if I went with you. I know you're not working *that* much! Linc doesn't work all the time like that and he's just as rich as you, if not richer. Now I got you back with your friend. How does that feel?"

Through fiery eyes, Randall studied her quietly.

Linc looked bothered by her words and apologized further. At one point, he reached for a towel to cover up. He never laid hands on it.

Randall's fist slammed into his jaw and his stomach. Linc buckled over and crashed against the shower floor. Fighting ensued, with mostly Linc trying to protect himself from Randall's rage. Selena's screams summoned Randall's brothers up the stairs and into the bedroom. They rescued Linc, rushing him out of the house and far away from Randall.

She took her time draping her slender body in a bathrobe. Randall knew that she wanted to humiliate him that much more by letting his brothers see her nude. Nevertheless, Jackson, Hunter, Tyler, and Dustin kept their distance from the bedroom, leaving them alone.

Selena plopped down on the side of the bed and smirked. "So how does it feel to be cheated on? It doesn't feel good, does it, Randall? I hate what you're doing to me! I know you've been cheating and I had to pay you back! No man works that much or goes on that many business trips! You think I'm a fool!" Tears glazed her eyes.

Randall observed her for several seconds. Abruptly he opened the briefcase that he had carried into the room, removed papers from it, and tossed them at her.

"What is this?" she asked, picking up the documents.

"The deeds to our mansion and the deed to the mansion I built for your mother."

Her mouth dropped open and her hand flew up over it.

"Look at them. Look at your surprise, my darling, *faithful* woman."

Frowning, Selena examined the papers. "Oh, Randall . . . I had no idea." She looked up at him. "I really had no idea. . . ."

"Well, let me give you some idea. If you're going to have something in this world, you're going to have to work for it. That's what I have been doing, breaking my back so I could have something in this life and give my bride and her family that joy, too."

She shook her head and a tear streaked her cheek. "I just didn't know. It just seemed like all those trips to St. Thomas were . . . And all that coming home late at night . . . I just thought you were getting it on with someone else. It's not my fault for thinking that way. Men have dogged me like that before."

"Don't give me that crap! Don't bring your baggage to me as an excuse for what you did. You were foul! I would never do anything like that to you. Even if you were cheating on me, it wouldn't even come up in my mind to cheat with your best friend to get back at you. My mind doesn't reach down in the gutter like yours obviously does. Now get out of my house!" He reached into the closet and tossed her clothes out of it.

Selena rushed up, grasping his hands, trying to make him stop. "No, Randall, don't do this! Please, let's try again. I love you. I love you so much and I'm so sorry."

"Get your hands off me."

She cradled his face. "But I love you."

"Get your hands off me! And get out of my house! I don't ever want to see you again. Get out!"

The next morning Randall called off the wedding and avoided Selena at every turn. Repeatedly Linc called him to apologize. Each time, Randall hung up on him. When he heard that Selena and Linc continued their affair, he knew he made the right choices in severing ties with each of them. How sorry could they have been when they continued sleeping together? Tonight, from Linc's own mouth, he even learned they had moved to St. Thomas together.

These days he couldn't have cared less if they slept together or not. He wanted nothing to do with either of them. His life had changed, especially lately. In the past few days, a hopeful spark for love lay in his heart. Jada caused that.

Chapter Ten

For the remainder of the workweek, Jada's infatuation with Randall flourished. Striving to dismiss her attraction to him became an arduous task. Often she sat back marveling at the way he treated people. Old-fashioned respect to the elderly tenants, and his humor with the children who frolicked on his villas' playgrounds, warmed her heart.

Randall was also courteous and down-to-earth in his interactions with those who worked for him, like carpenters, electricians, landscapers, and decorators. The CEO of a boys' club even called to thank him for his sizable financial donation. Everyone liked him. If only he knew to what degree she did.

On Friday, the end of the day approached. Jada hesitated going home because she wouldn't see Randall for the entire weekend. She wondered what he had planned later, along with Saturday and Sunday. Did he have a hot date? Did he plan to trot over to Cindy's place?

Jada feigned disinterest in what they did at Cindy's villa the previous night. Only she knew that she stayed awake most of the night tormenting herself with various mental scenarios. In all of them, she envisioned a wild-looking Cindy thrilling Randall with passion.

"Jada?"

Her head snapped up toward Randall, who leaned in her office doorway. "You need me to do something before I leave for the day?"

He strolled toward her desk. "I know you were about to leave to start your weekend, but I was just curious if you wanted to see the Sea Breeze Inn. You know, it's the place that Gus and I are rebuilding."

Jada restrained her happiness at the invitation, offering him a tiny smile. "I wouldn't mind seeing it."

"I know we kind of talked about you helping with the refurbishing of it," he went on, rubbing his chin, "so I wanted you to see what you were getting into. And I do plan to pay you extra for any work that you may do on the site, whether it's some type of physical labor like painting a windowsill, or clerical or management duties.

"I just appreciate your offering to help me. The hotel is going to take a lot of work. I plan to handle the business end and as much physical labor as possible. Maybe we can work side by side painting or something."

Her smile grew more sensuous. "Maybe so."

"All right, Ms. Gracen. Let's just close up here and we're off."

* * *

The Sea Breeze Inn looked nothing like Jada expected. She had imagined a dilapidated structure with wild shrubs and weeds besetting it. An attractive colonial-style, three-story hotel perched on a secluded beach was what she beheld.

Palm-shaded, the shoreline flaunted sugar-white sands with lush, jungle vegetation flanking it. As they strolled the distance to the building, Randall pointed at the wooded areas. He shared his plan for transforming them into parking lots for the lodge's guests.

Jada nodded, listening to his ideas, when unexpectedly the brilliant blue sky clouded. Shortly after, rain poured down. It was the strangest thing Jada had ever experienced. One second vibrant sunshine warmed their skin. The next second a downpour stole the luster of the day.

Randall and she ran inside the inn, laughing loudly like children. Once inside the lodge's quarters, they attempted to shake off the water. Their clothes were soaked.

Randall remembered he had a few shirts and jeans in the back of the Ford Explorer he had driven. "I'm going to run back out and get us some dry things."

"Get a move on it," Jada teased, watching him sprint out to the beach from the window. Once alone, she attempted to shake off the water again. A clammy feeling crept over her and she couldn't wait to change.

At least she felt comforted as she scanned her surroundings. Furniture-free, the lobby area looked like renovations had already begun. The palest yellow walls appeared freshly painted. Hardwood, cinnamon-hued floors shimmered as if recently polished. A toolbox shoved into a corner was the sole item within the room.

Randall returned seconds later. He carried two plaid shirts and two pairs of dungarees.

"Here, put this on," he said, handing her one of the shirts and slacks. "I know they are much too big. My brother Hunter and I threw them in the Explorer when we went on a fishing trip the last time he was on the island, but we never wore them."

"Thanks."

Reaching for the clothes, she gazed in his eyes and then surrendered to the temptation at his chest. His shirt lay soaked against it, making imprints of biceps that rose and fell with his suddenly rapid breathing. Drawing in a breath, Jada stared back in his eyes. She caught them roaming over her body, admiring every curve and crevice revealed from her drenched clothing. For a crazy moment, she longed for him to take them off her.

"I, uh, better go into another room and change," he said huskily as he looked back at her face, his eyes clinging to hers. "Then we'll, uh, take a tour of the place."

"It sounds good to me," she agreed, feeling stirrings at the base of her stomach.

Randall looked like he wanted to say something else to her. Instead he walked out of the room.

Jada pulled her wet top up over her head. All the while, she closed her eyes imagining that Randall removed it. She imagined that he removed everything from her body that so longed for him at this moment.

By the time she reached back to unclasp her bra, bare footsteps thumped behind her, freezing her movement. She made a motion to spin around.

Randall clutched her waist and pulled her back against him, thwarting her turn.

His fingers slid up and down the contours of her waistline and ribs, before they traveled along the curve of her hips. Jada inhaled sharply from the sweet invasion of such strong hands touching her that way. Soon his lips joined in the seductive madness that wreaked havoc on her. He brushed the sides of her face and neck, ravishing her.

"Oh," she whimpered, letting her head roll back against him, letting her entire body collapse against his solid frame.

Randall buried his face into her neck and kneaded his nose into her hot flesh. As he drank in her sensual scent, his lips slow danced from the bottom of her chin to the base of her throat. His arousal grew near unbearable. So long he had waited to do this.

Jada trembled through every lust-rousing second of him holding, kissing, and caressing her. Feeling his hands gliding around her from her sides to the front of her made her quiver far more. At her belly button, Randall sealed her against him. A massage began at her stomach. All the while, he continued bestowing her hot-blooded kisses along her neck.

Amid the frenzy of desire he incited in her, his fingers dared to climb. They made intoxicating motions upward to her breasts. His hands wandered inside her bra. Squeezing her, stroking her, and playing with her nipples with erotic expertise, he drove her crazy with sensual thrill after sensual thrill. She arched her chest forward, her body begging for more of what she couldn't get enough of.

Randall loved pleasing her. He hardened again

and again and again, seeing that he could make her climb the walls. He wanted to give her so much, all of him, his heart and his soul. He replied to her provocative request with more kisses along her neck that set him afire. Attempting to turn her on further, he palmed her lovely mounds while the other hand slipped down the front of her beyond her skirt.

"Open up," he whispered between kisses along her ear. His fingertips moved beneath her panties and played titillating games with her silken, coiled hairs. Breath lodged in his throat when he felt the rising tide of his need about to burst from him.

Crazed by the loving lavished on her, Jada clenched her thighs and the place between them moistened. With his every touch, she felt herself moving closer and closer to that cliff of no return. She craved for him to love her the way she had fantasized about all these years.

"Open up," he whispered again, his fingers nearing her secret place and soon causing tremors of ecstasy to flow through her.

Randall swung her around, searching deep inside her love-drugged eyes. "I waited so many years to love you like no other man can. Please let me love you right now."

Chapter Eleven

Randall pulled her into his arms. Swept against his excited, powerfully built body, Jada felt every part of herself weakening. The heated way he looked at her, the addictive way he smelled, his sweet ways toward her, and her emotions that grew with every second around him, all made her helpless when his mouth captured hers. Throughout each rapturous second that he kissed her, he eased her down toward the hardwood floor.

Jada couldn't believe she was about to make love to him and Randall was about to make love to her. Tasting him and holding on to his massive shoulders, she felt so sensually alive it was as if she were eighteen again, in his arms, in that moment, right before they were about to make love. But they had not made love, she reminded herself. He had left her and never returned.

"No," she said, pulling away, reaching for the dry shirt that she had let fall.

"Oh, baby, please," he protested in a voice low and laden with desire. "I want you and you know you want me, Jada. You know I wasn't being real when I said we didn't feel anything when we kissed. I know I felt something. I know you did, too. If we made love right now, it would be the most incredible experience each of us has ever had. What we felt years ago, it never went away. You know that."

Those words and how poignantly he expressed them touched her so much, she pondered them for several seconds. Desperately she wanted to believe Randall felt something powerful for her. Deep in her heart, she knew what she felt for him had never gone away, not even when he hurt her. Then again, just because her potent emotions had lived on didn't mean she had to succumb to them. She prided herself on being an intelligent woman. She had to be sensible.

"I'm not sure about us, Randall."

"I am. I'm sure of why our paths crossed again in this life. We were brought together for a reason, Jada. What we had when we were younger wasn't meant to end years ago. And I feel like all these years, I've been growing and making myself the best I can be, and now I can present that man to you. I've never been more certain of anything than I am about us. I know who I want and I'm looking at who I want—you."

She shifted her attention out the window, staring blankly at the beach and ocean.

"What are you thinking?"

A wistful smile tipped up the corners of her lips. "About tomorrow."

"What about it?"

"Tomorrow was supposed to be a big day in my life. It was supposed to be my wedding day."

"Wow," he remarked.

"Wow is right. My ex-fiancé, Michael, asked me to marry him on New Year's Eve, my birthday. And I accepted. I thought it was the most wonderful birthday and New Year's Eve I ever had. I just knew this time it was going to work out for me. Someone was going to love me forever—finally. But then only weeks after, he told me he slept with his ex-wife and they were getting back together . . . for the kids, he said."

"I'm so, so sorry, Jada. That was unfair to you. You don't deserve that."

"Well, that's what I got. But nothing like that will ever happen to me again. I won't allow it. Neither you nor anyone else will be given the chance to break my heart again."

"You're right. *I won't* break your heart. I want the chance to fill your heart up with so much happiness. I want to be your man again and treat you the way you deserve to be treated."

"What is the difference between what you did and what Michael did, Randall? There is no difference really. You both deserted me for another woman. You both just threw me away like I was nothing."

"That's not fair to me, Jada. I loved you. I explained the circumstances."

"Yes, you did explain. But it all comes down to me getting kicked aside. It all comes down to men hurting me. I'm so tired of it."

"No, this comes down to you giving your ex too much power. He hurt you and now you're not giving any other man a chance to love you. He's making sure you're not happy with any other man and that's because you let him. I felt the same way a short time ago. No woman was getting close to me again. But since you came back in my life, I feel differently. And you should, too. You shouldn't be putting the baggage that guy dumped on you in our relationship."

"Randall, our only relationship is friendship. And that's because I'm going to be strong by myself, doing for myself. That's what I've been taught to do. Do you know the women in my family have been cursed?"

He scowled. "What?"

"My grandmother, my mother, my sister, Katherine, and I are all alone because men walked out on us. It's a curse. But I'm not going to let it get me down. And I'm definitely not going to let what happened to Katherine happen to me."

"What happened to your sister?"

"It's a long, pitiful story."

"If it's something that upset you, I have all the time in the world to listen."

Abruptly Jada's eyes glazed and her expression grew more melancholy. "Her husband made her lose her mind. When they first started out, he was so nice to her. He had the whole family fooled. We thought he was the perfect man, too. He was a trustee in the church and a corporate executive at an advertising firm. They bought a house and had four beautiful children.

"Several years after the marriage, Katherine started calling us, crying all the time. She said that Al was staying out late and not taking care of his responsibilities with the family. Katherine had to use her nursing salary for all the bills and all the children's needs. But she loved him so much that she wouldn't let him go.

"But he wanted to go. He asked her for a divorce. When she said no way, he told her that he was having an affair and wouldn't stop seeing the woman. He told her that she didn't do anything for him anymore. But Katherine tried. She started getting her hair and nails done and wearing fashionable clothes. She started buying all these recipe books for his favorite meals and even buying these books on how to improve your sex life. But nothing worked. Then one day she came home early from her nursing shift. That *slimy* husband of hers had the other woman in their bed."

Relating to the situation more than he wished to, Randall shook his head. "There are some foul people out there."

"Yes, there are. Katherine went off. She tried to beat them both up. But Al told her this was what she got for not giving him a divorce. The woman was even laughing at her, telling her that she had taken her man. And Al, he pushed Katherine out of the room—out of her own bedroom. He told her to get out of his house. She refused to. So then he went in for the kill. He locked the door and he . . . he continued making love to the woman.

"Katherine was hysterical that her husband would be that cruel. Who would think anyone who had supposedly loved you could be that cruel? Katherine banged on the door, cursing them, then sat down and listened to them—listened to the noises of her husband making love to another woman. When Al and the woman finished, they came downstairs and found that Katherine had cut up her wrists. Worse than that, we saw that she had lost her mind."

"Jada, that has to be one of the most horrible things I've ever heard."

"Yes, it was horrible. Katherine went into the hospital and then later a mental facility. She was totally out of it. She didn't know her kids, me, my mother, or grandmother. All she kept saying was, 'Daddy's gone. Now Al has gone, too.' But I'm grateful that these days she's home and much better. She's not fully herself, but she's much, much better than she was. Little by little, she told us everything, too. She told us about that day she slit her wrists and told us about all the mental abuse her husband put her through."

"He was no kind of man, Jada. Her husband was a coldhearted animal. Surely you wouldn't think I could do something like that to you."

"Randall, I do know that you wouldn't be that cruel. But to tell the truth, nothing surprises me anymore. My daddy left. You left. Some of my boyfriends left. My husband left. Now my fiancé left. I'm just tired of it. If love is a game, I've lost so many times I don't have the spirit to play a round again."

"You're going to feel differently. Just give it some time."

"Why should I? I don't have to. Who says that every woman has to be with a man? All I need to do is be strong, seek my purpose, and not depend on a man—especially not on his love—because it never lasts."

"That's so sad you're thinking that way, Jada."

"It's not sad. It's smart. I'll never give a man my heart again."

"So what is this connection we're feeling?"

Jada avoided him by looking about the room. When their gazes fused again, she took a deep breath. "Randall, I need this job, but if I'm going to have to fight with you all the time, I might as well go back home and keep my peace. I enjoy the work and I'm falling in love with this beautiful island, but this . . . whatever it is between us is starting to be much more than I can handle. Now can you take me home please?"

"Sure. I'll take you home."

After Randall drove Jada to her villa, he lumbered into his own home shortly after. His maid was leaving and peered at him with concern. She asked if he was okay. He lied, telling her that he had never felt better. Once he was alone, he couldn't lie to himself.

Sprawling out on his beige leather sofa, Randall closed his eyes and visualized those sizzling moments with Jada. Recalling the minutes afterward, he opened his eyes. During the ride to her home, her silence had spoken volumes. It made him think.

Maybe he did need to stop pursuing her so intensely. Perhaps he needed to let it go and accept her friendship and role as an employee. On the other hand, he couldn't kid himself. When it came to Jada, passionate emotions possessed him. He could wish they would vanish all he wanted to. However, his past reminded him that they weren't going away. His feelings for her were as strong as they were years ago, if not stronger.

His contemplation drew him within it so greatly that the unexpected ring of his doorbell annoyed him. He wasn't in the mood for company; that is, unless Jada wanted to speak to him.

Chapter Twelve

Seeing Gus's chubby face in the doorway uplifted Randall. They strolled out onto the patio, sat at the table, and sipped beers while listening to the ocean swishing in the distance.

"Gus, do you remember that young lady I introduced you to days ago?" Randall took a swig of his Heineken and, smacking his lips, set the can back down. "The one who works at my management office?"

Gus wagged his balding head. "Who can forget her? She's beautiful. She's very exotic looking and seems nice, too."

"She is *very* nice. She is just as beautiful on the inside as she is on the outside."

Gus angled his head sideways, studying him. "When you introduced us, I remember you said you knew her a long time. Is she the same one you told me about years ago—the one you were in love with?"

"Yes, she is. Every day was so awesome when we were together."

"And you're in love with her now, too, aren't you?"

Randall took a deep breath, expanding his chest high. "All I know is that I feel the same way I did for her years ago. Sometimes it feels like it's even stronger. And I know she feels the same way." He thought of how passionately Jada had responded to him today. "Yes, she feels it, too."

"So that's a good thing, son."

"Not if she doesn't want to be with me that way."

"What do you mean?"

"I hurt her, Gus. You know the story I told you about Carolyn, and that I had to leave Jada back in Savannah."

"But come on, that was years ago. You were a kid. And it wasn't even your fault. The woman was pregnant with your child."

"Jada knows all that. I told her everything. But it's still hard for her to deal with. You know, me not coming back to be with her. Plus, she's had some hard times with men. I know I can be good for her. I know we can be so good together in every way. I *feel* it. But she won't give me a chance."

"Take your time, son. She'll come around. If she still feels the same way, she will come around. Remember, you just can't pick up where you left off years and years ago. Lots of things have gone on in both of your lives. Experiences have happened to both of you to change you and make you see life in different ways. You have to reintroduce yourself to her. You have to be her friend first. Don't force the romance. Let her get to know you as simply a man. Show her that you're a good man, worthy of her love."

Smiling, Randall patted Gus on the back. "You're all right, Gus. You're all right with me."

"Does that mean I'm a cool, older guy?" Gus joked.

"One hundred percent."

They laughed together.

"So does that mean you'll listen to me concerning another matter?"

"What other matter?" Randall asked humorously.

"Linc. He told me he ran into you."

The joy that lit up Randall's face instantly wilted. "I don't want to talk about him."

"Son, you have to face reality. You, Linc, and I purchased the Sea Breeze Inn together. Therefore, we're going to have to make a go of it together. We're partners."

"I am not working with him."

"So you're planning to bail out and sell your shares?"

"No way! I'm planning to get rid of him and run the hotel with you. I have talked to my lawyers about it."

"And I bet you they've told you that if he hasn't done anything improper in his business dealings with you, it's going to be nearly impossible to cut him out of this venture."

"Believe me, I'm working on it."

"I don't want you to work on it. I want us to do the deal as planned."

"Gus, how can you expect me to work with him after what he did?" He heard his voice rising and lowered it, realizing that he spoke to Gus and not Linc. "Put yourself in my shoes."

"Son, I don't want to argue about this. But I will tell you that I love both of you young men like my own flesh and blood. And I know Linc is truly sorry for what he did and he truly wants to work with you. More importantly, he wants to be friends again. And I want that for you two also. It would do my heart good to see you at least be civil to him again. Please think about it, Randall. Then we can proceed with the hotel renovations."

"I won't have anything to do with that man. And I mean it."

Nearby, in the vicinity of Randall's mansion, Jada lounged inside her villa, in a silk-draped bed. All the while she lay trying to sleep, she tossed and turned instead. Conflicting thoughts about Randall tortured her. She dialed his phone number to talk about what happened and her feelings. Yet when he answered, she hung up. What more could she say that hadn't already been said?

Facing a bright, sunny Saturday on the tropical paradise the next morning, Jada knew it wouldn't do her any good to sit around the house moping. After all, she would be thinking not only of Randall, but of the wedding with Michael that would never be. She showered, dressed, and headed out for adventure. It was about time for her to see this beautiful island.

For breakfast she dined at a restaurant along the eastern shore. Opening onto Sapphire Beach, the Seagrape was an eatery recommended in the travel brochures. She enjoyed light sea breezes permeating the air while she slipped mouthwatering Belgian waffles onto her taste buds.

Experiencing St. Thomas's famous cruise ships was next on her agenda. On her way to the harbor, she discovered the Dockside Bookshop. As she browsed through its well-stocked shelves, she dreamed like she had a thousand times before of having her own bookstore. It all made her think of long ago, when Randall had raided all the book nooks in Savannah with her. What fun they had.

After purchasing several Arabesque romances and the latest suspense novels, Jada strolled to the pier. She relished the salt-sprinkled air and loved the feeling of sun rays warming her skin. Breathtaking, she thought, gazing out at the aqua-colored sea. Cruising along was just what she needed to get her mind off of things.

Jada boarded a yacht called the *Quatera,* which toured the ocean for a few hours. When it docked, her appetite had been whetted to explore other cruise ships. She stepped in and out of several that weren't operating at the time. Then she wandered onto a boat that looked like someone's home. Modern furnishings in earth tones complete with a chaise longue, which had a man's black dinner jacket slung across it, assured her she had trespassed on private quarters. Jada flounced around to leave.

"Did you come here to see me? I hope you did."

A man's rich voice spun Jada around. Embarrassed, she faced a tall chocolate-colored man, flashing a pair of cherry-deep dimples. He stood with his hands in the pockets of his well-fitting black slacks, which went well with a white silk shirt. Shamelessly and unhurriedly, his dark, glistening eyes wound over her from head to toe.

"I'm sorry," Jada said. "I was looking for another tour boat and wound up here. The other boats aren't operating right now."

"I can take you where you want to go." He stepped toward her, extending his hand. "This is my yacht. I'm Linc. And who are you, fine lady?"

"Jada," she said, watching his head incline to her hand as he kissed it. She was taken aback by the flirtatious act and knew she would never take a ride with a stranger. She had to admit, however, he was very handsome. "Actually, I wanted to take one of the scheduled tours, so I can ask a lot of questions about different things."

"Maybe I can fill you in on things with my tour, and some dinner. I have a great chef on board."

The offer sounded tempting. Still, Jada knew it would be insanity to ride with a stranger, even one this charming. "It's really nice meeting you, Linc." She backed to the door as she spoke. "And thank you for the offer. But I really want to take one of the scheduled tours to learn about the island. But you have a good day." She exited the boat.

Linc hurried to the door and curved his head around the doorway, watching her walk away. "You have one, too. And please come back again."

Jada found another tour that was operating. She enjoyed it, made a few friends, and then returned to her villa at early evening. As she approached her porch, she saw Randall sitting on her steps.

She hid her surprise. "What are you doing here? Shouldn't you be on a hot date on a Saturday night?"

"No, no date. I just wanted to see you." He saw

her face frowning and knew she thought he wanted to pressure her again. "And I'm not here to hound you about us being together . . . as lovers. I'm here as a friend. Maybe I haven't been a friend to you. I've just been letting my attraction to you take over and not giving you a chance to know me again, and me to know you."

She sat next to him. "I do feel like I'm getting to know you. And I . . ."

"You what?"

"I think you're a very nice man, Randall. A good man, too. I can see why someone like Cindy would be throwing herself all over you. I bet she's a good cook, huh?"

He laughed gently.

She shot him a playful look. "What's so funny?"

"There's nothing going on with Cindy and me. I just made it seem like I wanted to accept her dinner invitation to make you jealous. It was childish and I apologize."

Relief washed over Jada that she dared not show. "You're right it was childish," she said with a lighthearted laugh.

"But just wanting to be your friend is not. I would like to spend some time with you, not as someone who wants to be your man, but as two friends just having fun on this paradise of an island. I would like to take you to dinner, sightseeing, dancing, whatever you want—but just as your friend. I won't make any move whatsoever on you—I mean unless you want me to. So how does that sound?"

Jada gazed across the courtyard in silence so long that Randall thought she would never answer him.

At last, she smiled at him. "That sounds real nice. Everyone needs a friend."

"You made my day," he said, looking in her eyes and then forcing his gaze to the shopping bag she carried. Books stuffed it. He pulled out a suspense novel from among the pack. "You must have read all the books I had sent to the office."

She shifted sideways, leaning back on the porch steps. "You know me and my books."

"I certainly do, young lady." He flipped through a number of pages and handed the paperback book back to her. "Looks like a page-turner."

She tucked it in her shopping bag. "I'm going to cuddle up with it and a nice piece of fried chicken tonight."

He was tickled. "Oh yes, I remember you with that fried chicken at Ms. Emma's. You would get up in the middle of the night and fry some. Had me even craving fried chicken in the middle of the night."

Jada laughed. "I sure did. I remember that. Everybody has their little weird thing. Frying me up a chicken back, or a thigh, in the middle of the night is mine."

He laughed heartily and watched her laugh and her eyes sparkle. He enjoyed making her comfortable like this and glanced back at the books in the bag. "So what about the bookstore? Are you still going to pursue your dream?"

A pensive expression seeped over her face, mixing with her smile. "One of these days."

"Ah, you can tell your boss," he teased. "I won't fire you because I know you're moving on to bigger and better things. I used to work for Gus at his development corporation, and all the while he knew that I planned to go out on my own. But he also knew that while I was with him, I gave him the best that I could. And that's what you've been giving me at the management office. Thank you for that."

She glowed. "You're welcome."

"So tell me what stopped you from making the bookstore happen throughout the years."

Her smile faded and she sighed. "Life. When I married, I worked and saved, but my husband's family always needed so much. And then Katherine had her breakdown and her husband vanished seemingly from the earth, and there was no one there for the kids. So I had to be there for them. Whatever they needed, I felt obliged to do. My savings for my bookstore dwindled away, but making those kids' lives easier and putting smiles on their faces was worth every penny I gave up for my business."

He stared at her with admiration. "That's beautiful. You have a good heart."

"What else could I do? I love those kids. They suffered enough having a father like that and seeing their mother out of her mind. Besides, I got something out of it—they love me just as much as I love them."

"And love *is* important," he said, knowing he felt the same way about his family. "I would do anything for my family, too. *Anything.*"

"I wish I had my store already, but I know I will have it one day. I'll have it when God is ready for me to have it."

His smile broadened and he shook his head.

"And what is so funny, Mr. Larimore?" she asked playfully.

"My grandmother, she used to say that. When we talked about wanting something, she would tell us that we will have it when God is ready for us to have it."

"It's true. I guess He didn't mean for me to have it these years. And to be honest, there were times I felt sad about it. Especially when I met one of my so-called friends. We would always run into each other at the mall. She always knew I wanted my own bookstore and every time I ran into her she would always ask me why I didn't have it. She would smirk when she asked it, almost as if it was funny that it never became a reality for me. Then when I was alone, I would feel sad."

"Jada, you know she was jealous. When someone is destined to do something big, there are some people who get jealous of that. She sensed the determination in you; and being your friend and knowing you, she probably knew how hard you would work until you achieved your goal. People like that sometimes don't have any dreams, or they don't have what it takes to make something happen, and they don't want you to have it either.

"But don't ever let what that woman said worry you again. She's not really a friend anyway. Your real friends will encourage you, and being a real friend, you will encourage them. And as your friend right now, I'm telling you, don't worry, Jada Gracen. It will happen in time. Your dream will come true. I know it will. And when it does, it may be in such a big and grand way, you would never have imagined it. As my grandmother also used to say, 'God has something special for you, girl.' "

Jada adored Randall's encouragement and as they sat talking about their dreams, experiences, careers, and various types of people they had met during their time apart, she cherished his knowledge and sensitivity as a person and a man. They conversed so much and so long, sunrise caught them.

For Jada, it felt like old times again. Whether at Ms. Emma's house or out touring Savannah, they used to talk for hours and hours. Though at the same time, their exchange tonight felt brand-new and exhilarating.

Randall had lived an interesting life and had so much to share. In turn, she didn't realize how interesting her life had been until she heard herself revealing it to him and he listened and responded with such interest. She wished she could have shoved the sunrise away and hold on to the precious hours with him forever.

Chapter Thirteen

In the succeeding two weeks, Jada felt like every moment was sprinkled with stardust. She and Randall accomplished many projects at work: getting more villas rented, meeting with vendors, and updating logs of income and expenditures. Lunches took them to posh restaurants that served Caribbean food, along with cuisine from other parts of the world. After work hours, they dined at restaurants with spectacular seaside views. As well, they spent countless "working dinners" at the oceanfront by his home.

On some occasions, they explored the beaches even though Jada couldn't swim and was too terrified of trying to let Randall teach her. Hence, he swam while she sunbathed. Magen's Bay Beach became their preferred of all the fun-in-the sun hot spots.

More daily excursions into paradise took them shopping at a number of boutiques in downtown Charlotte Amalie. Jada purchased luxurious items to send back home. Dancing at nightclubs and aboard cruise ships also filled their days with magic. Sightseeing at museums and famous Virgin Island tourist attractions made their time together delightful as well. With each moment around Randall, Jada felt not only her sexual defenses waning, but a love like she had never felt before growing so strongly inside her.

Every second spent with Jada, Randall put forth his best effort to restrain himself from taking her in his arms and making passionate love to her. He touched her with his message of love sent to her from his eyes. Somehow he felt more for her than he ever did. If only she would give in to what she felt. Each moment around her, her eyes touched him with a message, too. And when he lay down every night in his bed alone, he closed his eyes and saw hers looking at him, silently telling him, "I want you too, Randall. I'm in love with you."

One sweltering afternoon, when Randall headed out of the office to check on the construction of one of the villas, a knock at the door distracted Jada from the paperwork cluttering her desk.

"Come in," she invited the afternoon visitor.

Stepping inside the plush office space, Linc recognized Jada immediately. "Hello," he said with a beguiling smile. "I never thought I'd see you again."

Jada remembered the face. What woman wouldn't remember that face? Yet it took a few moments to recall where they had met. "The boat," she said finally. "That's where I know you from."

"That's right." He scanned the office and, impressed, shook his head. "Nice setup Randall has here. I assume you work for him."

"Yes, I do. Were you referred by someone? Are you looking to rent a villa from him?" She picked up one of the brochures Randall and she had created and handed it to him. "They are *so* luxurious. I live in one and love it. Would you like a tour right now?"

"No, I have a place to live, several places actually. What I wanted to see Randall about was another property, the Sea Breeze Inn. I also just wanted to talk with him. We're, uh . . . we're old friends. We go way back. Gus was a mentor to both of us."

Gus had come into the office many times during the last few weeks. Jada adored him. "Do you want to wait for Randall?"

"No, I don't have the time to wait around. I'll come back another time." He glanced at her ring finger, something he had not done in their fleeting moments on his yacht. "You're not a married woman who doesn't wear her ring, are you?"

She smiled. "No, I'm not married."

"Then would you like to have dinner with me tonight, on my yacht, or anywhere else you would like to go? We can even visit another island for dinner if you like."

Jada was flattered. "Thank you, but I have plans for the night." She thought of doing something with Randall—anything, as long as they were together. She had become addicted to his presence.

Inwardly Linc scolded himself. He had been so interested in getting with Jada, he hadn't considered the obvious: Randall might have been dating this gorgeous woman working for him. Then again, Randall had always been such a perfectionist about going by the books with his business. Clearly he recalled his buddy insisting that he would never date an employee or a tenant. That came about when one of their friends was accused of sexual harassment by his secretary, who had once been his girlfriend.

"Are you seeing someone?" he pressed.

Jada didn't know how to react to his boldness or to answer. "I'm having dinner with someone."

"He's a lucky man."

She turned on her computer. "I have some work to finish, but you can wait around for Randall."

"No, that's all right. I won't disturb you anymore. But I will most definitely see you again." His dark eyes lingered on hers. "I'll see you soon, Jada."

Over an hour later when Randall returned, filth and sweat covered him.

Jada trailed him into his office, noting that even unkempt that man was too sexy. "What happened to you?"

Randall plopped down in the chair behind his desk, grinning. "I had a ball. I was out there on the site, just getting down and dirty with the construction crew. I just love every aspect of this business. I was made for this."

Leaning in the doorway with her arms folded, Jada soaked up every drop of his boyish exuberance. "I'm glad to see you had such a good time, Mr. Larimore. You had a visitor while you were out there having so much fun, a friend of yours."

Randall folded his hands behind his head and

put his feet up on the desk. He crisscrossed them at the ankles. "Who came by? Gus?"

"No, Linc."

Straightway, Randall sat up. "What in the hell did he want?"

Jada noted the angry lines between his eyes and realized Linc had probably made Randall madder than anyone she had ever seen. "He wanted to see you about the Sea Breeze Inn and to see you because you're friends. You *are* friends, aren't you?"

"Hell no!"

Jada's brows rose at his tone. "Whoah, I better not get on your bad side."

"Oh, Jada, I didn't mean to snap at you. It's just that I have nothing to say to that man."

"What did he do?"

"Nothing to concern yourself with. It's not important. What are you doing this evening?"

"I'm not doing anything with you if you're going to carry this attitude with you."

Randall took a deep breath and gazed at her ruefully. "You're right. It's unfair to you to let this guy ruin a wonderful day and a wonderful night, too. I promise to forget all about him if you have dinner with me at my place."

"I would love it," she said, planning to find out more about his dislike for Linc.

On the balcony of Randall's mansion, Jada's and Randall's glasses were filled with red wine. Savoring butterfly chicken, Cajun shrimp, lobster, brown rice with chopped bacon, string beans, soft, sweet muffins, and salad, Jada inquired about his dislike for Linc. Reluctantly Randall shared that Linc and he had been friends and Linc had betrayed him.

"But how?" Jada grilled him.

"It doesn't matter how. All that matters is that he was like one of my brothers and stabbed me in the back. An enemy can hurt you, or a casual acquaintance, and you may get mad and sometimes even. But you shake it off and move on.

"But when someone you really, really care about hurts you—someone you welcomed into your life, hurts you—it's an excruciating type of hurt. It's not so easy to get over either. That's why sometimes you have brothers and sisters who haven't spoken for years. It goes that deep."

"I understand that type of hurt. People that I have loved have hurt me more than anyone." She lowered her head.

Knowing what saddened her, Randall raised her chin with his fingertips. "I know I'm included in those people, and I'm so sorry. But if I just had one chance to be . . . to be your man and love you, you would forget all that pain from the past, from every man, including me." He began caressing her cheek and his voice lowered to a husky whisper. "I know I said I would try to just be your friend, but I can't, Jada. You have no idea what I feel for you." He placed her hand on his chest to feel the hard, fast thumping she stirred within him. "I'm in love with you, Jada. More in love than I was before, if that's possible."

Jada's lips puffed apart with her astonishment.

The phone rang.

Randall ignored it, asking, "How do you feel about me now?"

She gazed at him tenderly, her heart racing.

The phone persisted in ringing.

"You better get that, Randall."

He stared at her a moment and left hesitantly. After speaking to Gus much longer than he desired to, Randall returned to the balcony. Jada had vanished. He called to her throughout the house. Soundlessness echoed back.

"What have I done now?" he mumbled with a sigh.

Randall concluded that he had scared her off again and she took a taxi home. Trudging up the stairs to his bedroom, he cursed himself for pressuring her again. All he wanted now was to jump into his bed and stay there for hours, wallowing in his misery. He had ruined everything again.

Then suddenly he heard the sound of the O'Jays' classic "Let Me Make Love to You" playing so lightly one could barely hear it. The music flowed from his master bedroom. When he walked inside the room, the alluring vision on his bed stopped him short. Jada sprawled across his bedcovers, looking nervous.

"Randall, I love you, too. And I want you to make love to me tonight. I want us to make up for twenty *long* years."

Chapter Fourteen

Randall sucked in a breath and his lips parted. Yet his voice remained lodged in his throat. He simply stared at Jada fully dressed on his bed, knowing that the pleasure of beholding her the way he had always dreamed of her stood seconds away. She had taken off merely her sandals. He knew he could handle taking off the rest.

Step-by-step as he walked toward the bed, Randall removed his clothing. Staring directly in Jada's eyes, he tugged at his tie and tossed it aside. He unbuttoned his white cotton work shirt and slid it off his arms. He pulled his undershirt up over his head. Now, bare-chested, he watched Jada's eyes wander over him. "I want you," she mouthed without even saying a word. Randall was too turned on. His breaths grew heavy with anticipation.

He ceased his footfalls just inches from the bed to rid himself of his pants. As he unzipped his zipper, he watched Jada biting her lip. When he removed his slacks and underpants together, her eyes enlarged and he heard her gasp. Her chest then rose and fell with her rapid breaths and she slid her foot along her leg as if she couldn't be still. He became more turned on, turning her on, and reached to his dresser for a foil package.

Jada watched Randall sliding on the rubber so sexily. Then she welcomed him as he came down onto the bed, his eyes still locked on hers. She couldn't help rising up and touching him. Cradling his handsome face within her palms, she marveled at it and glided her finger along his smooth lips. She dipped one finger inside his mouth. Slowly, he licked it with his eyes never leaving hers. The base of her stomach grew full with desire.

As she looked downward on his body, Jada's fascination led her to sliding her palm along his awesomely built chest and arms. Eyeing him, she dared to move lower, only stalling on his quivering stomach muscles.

"Go ahead, baby," he whispered, rubbing her hair. "Go on and touch me."

Jada couldn't help herself. Beautiful barely described how Randall looked. Extremely well-endowed, he was more than ready for her. Endlessly she had imagined how Randall would look without a stitch on. Her fantasies hadn't done any justice to this flesh-and-blood reality.

"You're a gorgeous man, Randall."

He gazed at her, his eyes drugged with sensual hunger. "I'm glad you think so. You're gorgeous, too. And I can't wait to make you feel beautiful. I can't wait to make you feel like you've never felt before. And I will do that once I'm inside you."

His words and their promise tantalized Jada. Her fingers probed beneath Randall's waist and she loved what she felt and how he groaned from her caress. As she gripped his hardness more firmly, he inhaled sharply before kissing her.

Gently Randall's mouth savored hers at first. As her touch grew bolder, stroking him feverishly, his mounting passion became urgent, unleashing its ardor between her lips. Deepening his kiss, he felt Jada's body quivering against his. Soon his hands roamed all over her.

Before Jada knew anything, Randall laid her down backward. His knees burrowed into the mattress and locked on either side of her thigh. Held so tightly within his grasp, Jada felt the place between her thighs throbbing. When he stared down at her for several seconds and then unbuttoned her top slowly, the pulsations grew. She writhed and her breathing grew loud. Her excitement was fed by the look in Randall's eyes. It was as if she turned him on like nothing else in this world. And that's what she planned to do.

Randall played with the frills on her top for a moment. He teased her by fondling the flesh on her chest, just above her breasts. When he saw she couldn't bear much more titillation, he took more pleasure in unbuttoning her blouse completely.

Cleavage bulged from a black satin bra. His nature hardened a thousand times over. Hurriedly he unclasped the back of the brassiere and slid it down her arms. Luscious, shimmering breasts stood be-

fore him with nipples so succulent he bent his head
to taste her.

Sensations washed over Jada that whirled out of
her mind. Her feminine heat pulsed with one jolt
of ecstasy after the other. Arching her chest forward to allow him total access, she wanted Randall
to do this to her forever. Each way she moved, his
tongue and hands discovered a new way of arousing
her nipples and entire breasts.

While he suckled, licked, squeezed, and kissed
her, Randall felt himself rising to another plateau
of erotic bliss. Anxious to fully love her, he unzipped her skirt and slid it off. His fingers shook
and his breath grew heavier as he tugged her red
lace panties down her legs next. He turned aside
to throw them on the floor. When he turned back
to Jada, she lay naked beneath him.

Randall rose up to stare at her. From head to
toe, his eyes drank in her sexiness. He had always
known she would look beautiful naked, but his
wildest fantasies couldn't compare to how hot she
looked lying on his bed. He grew so rock-hard that
he knew that if he didn't melt inside her soon, he
would burst from excitement before their bodies
even came together.

"I imagined how sexy you would look," he said,
skimming his fingertips over her breasts and dropping them to her lower stomach. "But my imagination is no match for you in the flesh. You're one
beautiful woman, Jada. And if you don't believe I
feel that way, let me prove it to you now."

He felt her trembling as he came down on her.
Mashing his hard body against her soft one and
feeling her arms come around him so urgently ex-

cited him to another degree. The fruit-scented lotion that she must have rubbed into her every pore stroked his senses pleasingly. He felt her hands caressing his back and backside, feeding his stimulation. He buried his face into her neck and collarbone, breathing in her sensuous scent. Anxiously he maneuvered his lips up to hers. His mouth moved across her plump lips in a titillating dance that packed another weight of steel into his manhood.

Nibbling her lips, he reached down, coaxing her thighs apart. His fingertips brushed and penetrated her wet petals, making her tremble and whimper. She moaned her extreme arousal into his mouth. He swallowed her passionate outcries with his kiss and cupped her backside. He withdrew his mouth from hers solely because the strain of foreplay had become too much for him.

Randall rose up and stared down at her. A light sheen of sweat covered her body, making her look even sexier. Caressing the silken inner skin of her thighs, his fingers soon spread them far apart. Closing his eyes tightly, he guided himself within her. The heavenliest wet warmth enclosed him. He groaned into her ear over, and over, and over, telling her how good she felt.

Clinging tight to his back, Jada cried out from the mind-blowing feeling of him pushing gently inside her. Barely she withstood the delicious sensations that he filled her with. The thickness and length of Randall overwhelmed her. As he thrust deeper inside her, for a second she wondered if he strove to pierce his way to her heart. But he was already there. Whether she wanted to or not, she loved him. She loved him like she had never loved any other man.

Intoxicated from everything about him and everything he did to her, Jada laced her arms around his neck and kissed his ears, begging for more. Randall obliged her with slow in-and-out movements. Wave after wave of red-hot bliss shot through her blood.

With his every motion, he whispered to her how good she made him feel, how sexy she was, and how much he loved her. Indeed, Jada had never felt more precious, desired, and thoroughly loved. Into his ears, into his chest, into his neck, she cried softly how much she needed him and that she was falling deeper and deeper in love. When his painfully pleasurable hip fluctuations became too much for her, she cried out loudly.

Greedily Randall covered her mouth with his, extracting all of the sweetness between her lips. At the identical moment, he cupped her backside beneath him and performed an excruciatingly erotic dance that caused her muscles to contract around him. He hardened a thousand degrees more.

Nothing had a right to feel so good, Randall thought. Among the hundreds of fantasies he had about Jada, never had he imagined she would feel like this. Never had he conceived that they would feel like this together. Every cell, nerve, and bone in his body erupted with unbearably blissful sensations. As unutterable ecstasy washed over him again and again, he groaned into her ear, begging her to keep doing what she did. Randall could never let it end.

Tenderly he maneuvered Jada onto her stomach. Propping pillows beneath her stomach, he positioned her for more red-hot love. He reached around to stroke her breasts with one hand, while the other hand placed his love inside her?

Back and forth Randall moved, making Jada cry out for his mercy. He kept up the red heat with more powerful strokes. But the rapture overpowered him. When he catapulted over heaven's cliff, he shook uncontrollably and felt Jada's limbs shuddering with his.

Spent, they lay perspired and entangled within each other's arms. Heavy breathing saturated the air.

Randall managed to say, "I love you."

Jada caught her breath. "Randall, I love you, too."

Smiling, he added huskily, "Did I make you happy?"

"Mm," she said with a lazy laugh. "Mm, mm, mm. Happy is not the word for it. There is no word for it. All I know is I have to have some more of you."

They made love many more times and in various rooms in the house. At the windup of their lovemaking on the living room floor, they fell into a deep slumber.

Both woke up in the middle of the night. It had become chilly. Randall carried Jada up to his bed and they snuggled there among candlelight.

"I'm so happy we're together," he uttered. "We *are* together, aren't we? I wasn't just a good piece, was I?" He grinned.

Jada threw her head back, laughing. "You are so crazy. No, you weren't a good piece. I told you I can't describe what you were. But I know who you are to me. You're my love."

"So does this officially mean I'm your man?"

"I'd be insane to let you go." She kissed his cheek.

He threw his eyes heavenward. "Thank you, Lord."

She giggled. "I wish we could spend every moment like we did last night, making love."

"Why can't we? I'm going to make love to you from the time I see you at the office until the time we're right back here in this bed. You see, romance doesn't start in the bedroom. It starts with all the wonderful things you do for the one you love to make sure she knows how special she is."

"You're so romantic, Randall."

"You bring it out of me. I want to share everything with you, Jada, your hopes and your dreams."

"I already love working with you. I love seeing you do your thing with the real estate. It's sexy the way you're so sharp and good at it."

"You're the sexy one." He pecked her on the lips. "And I'm going to make all your dreams come true."

"A big one sure came true tonight," she said with a chuckle. "That's for sure."

"You're fresh," he teased.

"And I'm going to be even fresher after being with you tonight. So watch out for your butt in the office. It's likely to get pinched."

He smiled to that and held her until she faded off into slumber. Cuddling her close to him, Randall basked in the memories of the passion they had shared during the night. He wanted more and he wanted to make her the happiest woman alive.

He intended to make her every dream come

true. She had done so much for the sake of her family. She deserved someone to have something done for her. He pondered that until he fell asleep.

Chapter Fifteen

The next morning Jada slept late while Randall hummed around in his kitchen gathering utensils and food to cook her breakfast. When the phone rang, he picked it up with the hint of a song in his voice.

"What are you so happy about?" his brother Hunter asked.

Randall searched in the cabinet and took out a container of grits. "Everything."

"Everything like what?"

"And good morning to you, too."

"Good morning, bro. Forgive my manners. But I know you have a woman there."

Randall chuckled and opened the refrigerator. "So what if I do?"

"All right, now," Hunter said in a roguish tone. "She must have really put it on you to make you sound like *that*."

Randall laughed. "Man, it's too early in the morning to be talking to you. You're crazy."

"Come on, bro. Give me some details."

"I'm not talking to you about my baby."

"Baby!" Hunter nearly choked on the word. "You're calling a woman *baby?* Man, you sound like you're about to turn in your player card. This is serious."

"You're the only player in the family. You're the one chasing all the skirts. I always wanted one good woman."

"That'll never be me. There are too many women out there to settle down with just one. I don't know what's happening to my brothers. First Jackson and now you're losing it. It must be something in the water. I'm sure not drinking any of it."

"All right," Randall said teasingly, "you keep talking that stuff. One of these days you're going to meet a woman that makes you eat those words."

"Never. Where is your *baby* anyway?"

"She's sleeping. I'm fixing her breakfast."

"Breakfast! You're fixing her *breakfast,* too? Man, when did you start cooking? Mom always tried to teach you how to cook and you would run and hide somewhere. And the last time I tasted something you cooked, it was so greasy that it hurt my stomach. Please don't make the woman sick."

"My food is not going to make my baby sick. I'm fixing her a traditional Southern breakfast with eggs, grits, sausages, and biscuits, and she's going to love it. I have cookbooks right by my side."

"Where did you meet your *baby* anyway?"

"It's Jada."

"Jada! Your Jada? The Jada that you left back in Savannah a long time ago when Carolyn had that accident?"

"Yes, Jada is back in my life. Isn't that beautiful?"

"It's great. How did you two hook back up?"

"Kelly and her matchmaking."

"That figures."

"She sent Jada here for the management position I had open. Neither one of us knew we were going to see each other either. She thought Uncle Nelson was interviewing her and I thought one of the ladies from home was coming to interview with me."

"That is something. Kelly needs to hook me up with some old girlfriends. So is she still fine?"

"She's beautiful in every way. You'll get a chance to meet her."

"So you're planning to bring her home, too? Now I know this is serious. You're going to be just like Jackson, messing up the players' club."

"I was never in the players' club. I am a one-woman man."

On and on the brothers chatted. They also discussed their family, Randall's villas, and Hunter's business. At the end of the conversation, Randall had to share the one dim spot in his life lately: Linc.

"You were bound to run into him since you two bought that hotel with Gus. Plus, the man bought boats and other property down there."

"You should see him up in my face, trying to make nice."

"Don't fall for it, bro. Any friend that sleeps with your woman is as low down as they come. And he is likely to do it again. Keep your new lady away from him."

"Jada wouldn't even waste her time. She's nothing like Selena."

"So what are you going to do about your business with him?"

"I have my lawyers on it. They're trying to find a reason to make him sell his shares."

"So how does that look?"

Randall sighed. "Not too good to be honest. He hasn't done anything shady in his business dealings with me, so it's very hard to get him out of it."

"That's rough, bro. Having a business with a man who slept with your woman is no joke. But you'll figure out what to do. You always do."

Hours later, Randall proved his brother wrong about his cooking skills. He served Jada in bed. She gobbled up everything on her plate and asked for seconds. Love was something else, he thought. Because of her love, he had learned to cook.

Jada and Randall enjoyed each other in his mansion for more than a few days making love. Demands at the management office dragged them from their love nest much sooner than they wished. Reluctantly they headed into the office and attempted to catch up on their workload. At the end of the day, Randall strolled home with Jada, sprinkling her face with kisses and telling her how much he appreciated her. When she opened the door to her villa, he proved every word he professed. Red, yellow, white, pink, orange, and lavender roses splashed their bright colors at every corner and crevice of the room.

She gaped at Randall, who stood rubbing his chin and grinning. "You did this, didn't you?"

"Not me," he teased. "They must be from one of your admirers."

"You did do it," she said, leaping up on him, lacing her arms around his neck.

The force of her jump made him stumble back on the couch.

She straddled him. "Randall Larimore, what are you doing to me?"

"Loving you, baby," he whispered. "Giving you all that I got." His hands slid up her back, drawing her deep into him. He sat up, seeking her tongue hungrily.

Before long, Randall carried her up the stairs to her bedroom. Curious about what he planned to do, Jada questioned his intentions repeatedly. In silence, Randall carried her to the bed and laid her on it softly. After removing his shoes and shirt, he took off her shoes and skirt. Next he rolled her panties off her legs. Randall coaxed her back and began kissing her belly. Finally he looked up.

"I want to do something just for you. I don't want you to do a thing. Just lie back and enjoy."

Jada laced her fingers through his hair as his head went lower and lower on her body until he reached her secret place. He buried his face into her silken patch, before his lips kissed her ever so tenderly. "Oh," she cried breathlessly. "Oh, Randall."

"Yes, baby, I'm here to make you happy."

Nights later, Jada had just hung up the phone, finishing a long conversation with her family in New Jersey when she noticed the clock on the wall. It read 8:30 P.M. In an hour, she intended to head downtown to Club Manderville. Randall and she had planned a night of dancing and fine dining at the swanky establishment.

Due to a business meeting that ran late, he had telephoned, telling her that he wouldn't be able to make it to the hot spot for its opening time. Despite that, he asked Jada to get there as they had intended. Club Manderville maintained a jam-packed house. Patrons obtained tables on a first-come, first-serve basis. If they both arrived tardy, they would be among the many who wouldn't be seated for the entire night. Jada refused to stand up and dance for hours in those high-heeled sandals she had just bought.

One of the hottest nightspots on the island, Club Manderville featured soul, jazz, pop, and Caribbean music. Jada couldn't wait to get there. It had been a long time since she had spent a carefree night shaking her booty around the dance floor.

The nightclub had been Randall's idea. From the breakfast he prepared her, to the roses, and all the little gifts he had showered her with in the last few days, he was intent on pampering her. Pampering suited her just fine.

Jada showered. As the water poured down over her shapely form, she thought of her conversation with her family. Because she had sent money back home for all their bills, they sounded peaceful, unworried, and happy. They told her that she sounded ecstatic and demanded to know what had happened in St. Thomas.

Because of the fiasco with Michael, they didn't dare entertain the thought of her getting involved with a man so soon. So her revealing her new relationship shocked everyone. Her mother and grandmother interrogated her about Randall. They also admonished her to get to know him before anything serious happened.

To that, Jada laughed to herself. If only they knew how serious they had been for these last days. Yet she told them not to fret. Randall Larimore was more than a man she met in St. Thomas. He was *the one.*

Jada emerged from the steamy shower mist into her bedroom's cool air. The difference in temperature hit her full force. Quickly she patted the towel over the water pellets on her skin and then grabbed the lotion from the dresser. With a tap of the bottle's head into her palm, the mixed fruity fragrance formed a pinkish liquid circle in the midst of her hand. Jada plopped down on the side of the bed.

Thinking of Randall, she rubbed the lotion along her feet, calves, thighs, stomach, chest, arms, and neck. She imagined Randall taking pleasure in kissing it all away later. That made her smile.

In a matter of minutes, Jada shimmied into a black, flared dress that stopped about three inches above her knee. In the mirror, she twisted and pranced around to get an idea of how the fabric would swing when she danced. On her face, she applied a fuchsia-berry lipstick, eye shadow, and blush. She styled her hair wild and loose. Seconds later, the limousine Randall sent for her whisked her away.

Jada had a short ride to the club. Instantly she realized why Randall wanted her to go ahead to secure a table. Scores of people hung around the outside of Club Manderville. Some conversed in groups. Others simply stood bobbing their heads to the funky music and checking everything and everybody out. Once she managed to get past the high-security-manned doors, getting a table proved to be a huge task. Fortunately she snagged one of the last available ones.

She waited for Randall at a half-hidden table with a candle lit in its center. Its flame emanated a raspberry scent. Jada found the scent so appealing, it seemed near edible. For her table, she ordered sparkling cider. Sipping it from a champagne glass, she bobbed her head to Musiq's latest dance groove. Jada had longed to get his latest CD. After hearing this song, she would definitely put it on her must-have list.

During the time she tried to kill time, companionship never lacked. Man after man dropped by her table. Continuously, Jada repeated, "I'm waiting for my boyfriend. He should be here at any minute."

Eventually the music's tempo wound down. Jada observed couples getting on the floor to slow drag to the classic ballad "The Closer I Get to You." Jada relished the song. It lay stashed in her collection of favorites at home. She wondered what took Randall so long. She longed to cling to her man and sway their bodies to this spellbinding tune. She settled for swaying her head and mouthing the words.

"I like this song, and from that dreamy-eyed way you're looking, you do, too."

Jada looked aside and up at the familiar voice addressing her. Linc stood above the table dressed in a dark suit exquisitely cut to fit his robust body. Smiling, he stretched out his hand out to her.

"Hello, Linc," Jada greeted him. "I'm waiting for my boyfriend."

"That's all right," he said, still extending his hand down to her. "We're just going to be dancing. We're not making love." His eyes lingered on hers with those last words.

Chapter Sixteen

Jada smiled at him and hoped she didn't look as awkward as she felt. She started to tell Linc that Randall was her boyfriend and he disliked him. Therefore, she would shun dancing with him.

Then again, Randall hadn't even told her what ticked him off at the man. It was silly for her to be fuming at Linc without justification. Slow-jamming with him was better than sitting around waiting to be hit on by guys. Besides, she could never hear enough of this mesmerizing ballad. The thought of dancing to it thrilled her.

Donny Hathaway's ultrasoulful voice crooned away. He serenaded the object of his affection, expressing that he tried to be only her friend, just as Linc escorted Jada to the dance floor. Soon Linc's body fitted to hers and they moved slowly to the haunting melody.

Linc behaved very gentlemanly at first. Skillfully he held Jada at a distance that allowed their bodies to barely brush. However, as the song progressed to the succeeding verse, his embrace grew stronger.

Linc's sturdy hands slid up and down her back, dragging out their probe at the bottom of it. Then he drew her closer to his body. So close that Jada felt something on him that she shouldn't have. It made her uncomfortable. It made her rethink her decision to slow-dance with him.

No, Randall had no right to control her. He had no right to tell her whom to dance with. On the other hand, for some reason, he disliked Linc. Certainly he wouldn't appreciate Linc holding her and dancing with her like this. And God forbid if he knew how stimulated Linc had become.

Jada leaned toward Linc's ear to tell him that she didn't want to dance anymore when suddenly she heard him say, "How you doing, my man?"

Jada threw her gaze over her shoulder to see whom he spoke to. Her heart flew up in her throat. Randall stood right beside them. He avoided her face. He glared at Linc.

"Hey, baby," she said, turning to him, touching his chest.

Stern-faced, Randall moved around her and shot at Linc, "What do you think you're doing?"

Linc, realizing that Randall was her boyfriend, retreated a few steps. It had crossed his mind that Randall might be her man. Yet he shook off the thought just as easily as it had come. Randall had high standards in regard to not dating employees.

"Look, man, I meant no harm or disrespect. We were just dancing. I—"

In the span of Jada's blink, Randall's fist lunged forward; Linc went down to the floor.

With a fierce look in his eyes, Linc got up and appeared like he wanted to charge back at Randall with a pounding of his own. Rather than that, he wiped the line of blood that seeped down from the corner of his mouth and walked away. Within seconds, he had disappeared among the crowd.

Randall then grabbed Jada's hand and pushed his way through the swarm of dancers packing the floor. Shortly after, they sat in his Mercedes.

"I cannot believe you did that," she said as he started up the engine. With a huff, she crossed her arms and shook her head. "I just can't believe it."

"What can't you believe?" he asked, dropping his hand from the ignition, scowling across at her. "That I knocked his butt out?"

"No, that you're such a brute, Randall! You love to fight, even when you were a kid. I remember how you beat up that guy in the restaurant that time. It was pitiful."

"Don't you want a man who can protect you?"

"Of course!" she screeched. "But I don't want my man going around beating up innocent people!"

A curt laugh escaped him. "Linc is far from innocent."

"Oh, come on. Why did you hit him like that? We were just dancing."

Randall shifted his body to face her fully. "My enemy has his hands all over my woman and I'm not supposed to do anything?"

"Randall, he didn't have his hands all over me,"

she said with a high pitch. "We were just killing time while I waited for you. He didn't even know you were my man."

"If he didn't then, he knows now. You shouldn't have danced with him knowing the way I felt about him. You have no loyalty. I'm surprised at you."

"Oh, please." She frowned at him, still shaking her head. "I'm surprised at how you're acting. What did Linc do to you anyway? You really have me wondering now."

Randall peered into his rearview and then adjusted his side mirrors. "I don't want to get into that with you. Just stay away from him."

"Did your falling-out have to do with business?"

"Huh," he remarked, pulling into traffic. In an offhanded way it did, since they parted ways with business and all else after Linc and Selena betrayed him. "You can say that," he answered her.

"My God, then tell me, what did the man do? I'm so curious now. Did he steal some money that wasn't his? I hear a lot about business partners doing that to each other and then the friendship is over. They wish they never would have done business together."

Randall kept his eyes on the road. "I don't want to talk about him."

"What do you want to talk about then?"

"Nothing, all right?"

They rode in silence all the way to his home. Even after he parked the car and she trailed Randall toward the ocean setting behind his home, he had little to say. Beneath the moonlight, they sat in silence. Waves crashed against the shore and they watched them. Relaxed on the sand, Jada curled her legs to the side. Randall sat with his legs bent and his arms locked around them.

Every so often, Jada looked across at Randall's handsome features. They displayed more somberness than rage. And suddenly she could feel what he felt. She wouldn't have liked him dancing with someone whom she detested either.

"I'm sorry," she apologized. "I shouldn't have danced with Linc. It was wrong of me to do that with someone who has obviously done something terrible to you."

Randall's gaze remained on the dark, galloping waves. "Did you enjoy it?" he asked so quietly that the sound of the ocean swishing nearly drowned his voice.

The question made Jada ponder the last part of her dance with Linc. It had become more uncomfortable than fun. Yet she didn't dare tell Randall that or why she felt that way. She just wanted their first quarrel to end. "Dancing with Linc was okay." She shrugged her shoulders. "It was just dancing. I would have preferred dancing with you."

Still facing ahead of him, Randall took a deep breath. "Are you attracted to him?"

His jealousy unnerved Jada. At the same instant, she noticed the downheartedness on his face. Guilt overcame her. "Baby, you're the only one I want. Let me prove it to you."

She touched Randall's shoulder. He ignored her, his eyes still riveted on the sea. Jada stood and sashayed behind him. She hoped he would follow her. He didn't. She remained behind him for several seconds before uttering, "Baby, turn around."

Taking his sweet time, Randall looked back over

his shoulder. What he beheld caused him to draw in a breath. Naked, Jada sprawled on her side in the sand. Her elbow was propped on the shore and her palm lay against her cheek.

Languorously, Randall took in every inch of her. When he finished, his head turned from side to side as he scoped out the area.

"I already looked, Randall," she whispered. "There's no one out here tonight but us. It's the perfect place to prove how much I love you."

Still hush-mouthed, Randall crept toward her. His lips crushed against hers while his hands divided their special treatment between her nipples and the silky coiled hairs far below them. A rush of red heat seized his manhood. His heart raced, and beholding how sexy she looked, he had to have her. Eagerly Randall shed his clothes and removed a foil package from his pants pocket.

Once again her mouth became the object of his obsession. As he kissed her passionately, his hands were equally merciless with his touch. His fingers feathered along her waist and up the curvature of her hips. He rubbed her legs, unable to get enough of their shapeliness and silkiness. When he reached her thighs, he stroked the delicate inner skin before his fingertips played with the honey between them. Randall's hard body solidified another rung, and he became more excited watching her hips rise as she sought more satisfaction from him.

His fixation became her breasts again. Unhurriedly he glided his tongue along them, dallying about her hardened nipples before trying to swallow them whole. Jada shuddered and moaned beneath him while he spread her legs far apart, preparing her for his ultimate love gift. Then in one careful thrust, he pushed his loving inside her.

"Baby, show me how much you love me," Randall whispered, his moist mouth kneading her ear. "Do what you want to me."

Jada could barely speak over their bodies' smoldering contact. All she could do was receive him, her hips leaping up from the sand because of the fire he unleashed within her. When she felt him going as far as he could go, his sudden stillness forced her own. They reveled in that pure feeling of being one.

She heard Randall let out a groan and felt him sway his hips wildly. Jada met his moves with equally salacious ones. Soon her burning need compelled her to do more. With sensuous body maneuvers, she eased Randall beneath her.

Caressing his strong shoulders and then kissing him, she rode him with a fever that caused him to holler out as if in pain. With it, over and over, she told him how much she loved him and that no man could make her feel this blissful but him.

Pumping him, she kissed his ears, whispering that he would be the only man to feel her love and that she would ache for his forever. When their rising tide had risen too high to bear, their bodies succumbed to the unbearable joy. Spasms shook them and Jada collapsed against him. He wrapped her tight within his strong arms.

"Baby," Randall said, barely able to catch his breath.

"Hmm?" she said lazily.

"If you ever want to work out a problem again in

the same manner, I'm more than willing to help you out."

To that, Jada laughed until she fell asleep.

Miles away, on his docked boat, Linc relaxed on a chaise so deep in thought, he didn't realize he hadn't locked his door. When his buddy Ozzie stepped aboard, it startled him.

Ozzie, whom Linc hired to work on his yacht and properties when he first arrived on the island, had been a constant companion. He had even introduced Linc to his sister.

Ozzie, a big, greasy-looking man with picture-perfect teeth, grinned at Linc. "Who kicked your butt, man? The guys told me a guy knocked you out in the club. So I had to see this swollen lip they told me about. It looks pretty bad."

Linc patted a cold towel on his sore lip. "Thanks for making me feel better."

Ozzie took a seat on the floor. "Aw, man, I'm just messing with you. Who was this dude anyway?"

Linc took a deep breath. "An old friend."

"No friend of mine kicks my butt like that."

"You sure are making me feel better."

"I'm just kidding with you, man. Lighten up. But seriously, if you want me and the guys to take care of this cat, tell us where he is. We'll rough his rump up. Throw him in the river, too, for the right price."

Linc arched a brow. "I know you're not saying what I think you're saying."

Ozzie threw his head back, laughing. "You know I'm just kidding and messing with you, man." He slapped Linc on the knee. "What he hit you for anyway?"

"His woman."

"You screwed her?"

"Not this one."

Grinning, Ozzie ran his tongue along his lips. "You screwed another woman of his?"

"Man, I don't want to talk about it. I was wrong before and he served me tonight for it. So this should be the end of it."

"How were you wrong? A woman wanted to give you some and you're supposed to turn it down? Hey, not me, and not in this life."

Linc shook his head at him. "No, man, I was wrong. I should have just left her alone. It didn't work out with us either."

Ozzie's bright eyes narrowed as he thought. "Was it Selena? The chick you came to the island with, the one with those big boobs?"

"Man, I told you I didn't want to talk about it."

"So it was her. Hell, I would screw her, too, if I had the chance. If you're really done with her, where is she? You wouldn't mind if I had my turn, would you?"

"I don't know where she is," Linc stated. "And yes, I would mind."

Ozzie laughed and the sound echoed as if it came from somewhere far. "Ah, that's okay, man. You're my man whether you want to share or not. And speaking of sharing, do you have fifty dollars you can loan me?"

Without a thought, Linc reached in his pocket and pulled out a hundred-dollar bill.

Ozzie's eyes lit up. He tucked the bill in his back pocket. "Thanks, man. I'm going to go find me a nice lady and treat her to a good time."

"What about your wife and kids? I assumed you wanted it to buy them something since you can hardly find any work."

"A man needs his playtime. Don't you agree?"

Chapter Seventeen

The next day, Jada and Randall locked themselves in his house, making love, eating delicious food, and watching movies. After seeing a movie in which a young woman reunited with her long-lost father, Randall gazed down at Jada, who cuddled against his chest, while they lounged on the sofa.

"Baby," he said, mingling his fingers in her tousled locks. "Do you ever see your dad?" Silence hung in the air so long that he wondered if she would ever answer. "Did I say something wrong?"

Jada looked up at him and forced a smile. "No, you didn't. It's just me. I try not to think of my father."

"Have you seen him lately? I remember the relationship was strained."

"It's worse than strained," she said with a strange laugh. "It's nonexistent. I haven't seen that man since I was a teenager. I don't even know where he lives anymore. We can't get in contact with him and he couldn't care less about getting in contact with us."

Stroking her hair, Randall thought for a moment. "It's not your fault, Jada. You did nothing wrong. It's him. Remember I used to tell you that? It's him, not you."

"I remember. I tell myself that, too. But sometimes, even as a grown woman, I still wonder that maybe I did something to make him stay away from me and not love me."

"Your father loves you. Don't think that way."

"I'll try not to."

Randall tried to brighten her spirits by taking her to Sapphire Beach. She simply wanted to sunbathe. But he tried to teach her how to swim like he always did. Jada did make some attempts this time. In spite of these, she failed to get the rhythm of swimming. Randall knew she had fun anyway. The body kisses that he gave her while he tried to teach her kept her smiling.

Arriving back at Randall's place, Jada headed to his bedroom and fell asleep quickly. Meanwhile, he raided the cabinet for some Lay's potato chips. As he sat in the kitchen crunching them, he couldn't shake off their earlier conversation about her father.

He hated the guilt Jada felt about her father's desertion. It all led him to his study, where he searched through his Rolodex. When he located the number of a private investigator whom he'd hired once before, he placed the card at the front of his desk. First thing in the morning, he planned to give him a call.

* * * *

A week later, Randall had located Jada's father, Paul. He had been living in Chicago, but relocated to North Carolina in recent years. Telling Jada that he had a business meeting in the Big Apple, Randall took an early-bird flight to visit her dad during the week. He was a custodian at a church. Randall met up with him on his lunch break.

Sitting among the vacant church pews, Paul Gracen bit into a sandwich and sipped a can of Sprite. When he saw the younger man joining him on the bench, he acknowledged him with a nod of his head.

"Can I help you?"

"I think you can, Mr. Gracen."

Paul's small eyes sharpened, scrutinizing the sharply dressed man among the church's orangey radiance. "You're a member of this church?"

"No, I'm a friend of your daughter Jada."

The numerous furrows on Paul's cocoa-brown face deepened. "What has happened to my daughter?" His chest heaved violently. "Is she all right?"

Witnessing the man's concern, Randall felt relieved. He wasn't a monster; he did love Jada. "Your daughter Jada is doing wonderfully."

The man exhaled. "Thank the Lord." Then suddenly he eyed Randall suspiciously. "So what do you want? How did you know where to find me?"

"My private investigator found you."

Paul's lips balled in an angry knot. "Child support, huh? Coming after me for the years I missed paying."

"Is that the first thing you think of when you think of your daughter?" Randall yelled, uncaring that he spoke to a man likely his father's age. "It's men like you who make women think bad of all of us men!"

Paul waved him off. "Get out my face, boy."

"Not until I finish my business with you," Randall said, normalizing his voice.

"Take it. I don't have much, but they can take it all. Money doesn't mean anything to me anymore."

"I'm not here for your money. I'm here because I want to bring Jada to see you, and I want you to tell her that you love her. Because I know even though you deserted her and her sister, you have to feel something for your own child."

Paul looked away from Randall. His line of vision aimed at the choir stands, but he saw a distorted view of them because of the water blurring his sight. He sniffled. "Boy, this is none of your business."

"It is when the woman I love is hurting because of what you did."

Paul shifted his gaze away from the choir stands, but he felt too ashamed to look Randall in the eyes. "Of course I love my daughter," he admitted with a sob. "I love both of my daughters."

"I'm so happy to hear that. Because she feels that you don't. And she also feels that maybe in some way she was to blame for your leaving."

"Aw, no," he said in an alarmed tone. "It had nothing to do with her or Katherine. It really didn't have anything to do with my wife, Mary, either. It was me. I made so many big mistakes and strayed so far from my family, I didn't even know how to come back anymore. When I did try, my wife didn't want me. But I can't blame her."

Randall continued listening as Paul opened up to him. When the older man concluded his story, Randall was certain he had done the right thing in feeling Paul out to see if he could reunite with Jada. Paul had made plenty of mistakes. However, he was extremely remorseful about the wrongs he had committed.

Randall hoped that when he brought Jada to see him, her father could communicate those sentiments to her. Sometimes it meant so much just to know that someone was sorry for mistreating you.

Days later, Jada accompanied Randall to North Carolina. He lured her away, telling her about a big surprise. After arriving in a quaint Southern town called Brooksville, he escorted her to a moderate-sized white-frame church. Inside it, he led her into a chapel that at first appeared empty. But it wasn't barren, she soon realized. She beheld a gray-haired man whose wrinkled face vaguely resembled her father's.

As she stood face-to-face with him again, Jada's hand flew up to her mouth and she froze in her footsteps. "Daddy?"

"How you doing, baby?" Paul said, smothering her within his arms. "You look good. Real good."

Randall tapped Jada's shoulder. "I'll be right outside, baby. If you need me, just holler."

She observed Randall walking out of the chapel and then switched her interest back to her father. Her parents were the same age. Yet her father looked ten years older than he actually was. And her mother looked ten years younger. Everyone complimented her mother's youthful appearance. Jada reckoned it proved that doing the right thing was good for the soul and doing wrong made for a hard life.

Paul asked her about the family and told her that he had relocated from Chicago because he received a job offer in this town. Jada talked mostly about her career and the wonderful position she had working with Randall.

"That boy cares about you so much," Paul said, smiling. "He came all the way here and tracked me down. Now, that's something. I'm glad you're with a good man."

"You are?"

"Of course, baby girl."

"Then why weren't you a good man to Mama?"

Paul hung his head. "That's a hard story. I told your boyfriend. He'll tell you."

"I don't want him to tell me, Daddy. I want to hear it from you."

Paul nodded and held on to her hand. "I love you and Katherine. I love you both so much."

Tears formed in Jada's eyes. "I never heard you say that before."

"I'm saying it now. I always loved you girls. You're my babies."

"So how could you just go off and forget about someone you love?"

"I never forgot about you or your sister. I think about you two every day."

"Then how could you do what you did to us? You stopped visiting us. There were no birthday cards or Christmas presents from you. You stopped sending money to take care of us. I used to feel so sorry for Mama working all those extra shifts and even extra jobs just to take care of us. And I would just imagine that you were off somewhere kicking your heels up with Helen, Mama's friend, spending money on her while we struggled to eat and pay the mortgage."

"I'm sorry" broke from him with a sob.

"Why? Just tell me, why?"

"I was wrong, Jada. Lord knows I was wrong. Your mama, she's a good woman. But I didn't know that at first. I thought she was nagging me when I would lose a job and she would be on me to get another one. Then if I wasn't making enough money at one job, she would tell me to go back to school. She even told me that if I went to college she would help pay for it and get an extra job. Now, the only kind of woman that will say that to you is a woman who loves you. She wanted to work together with me. But I felt she was nagging. And I also felt she was trying to take my manhood away.

"So when that Helen, her so-called friend, started coming on to me, I kind of felt that I was getting back at your mama. Like it served her right after her bothering me like I wasn't a man. That's what it was with Helen: she made me feel like I was a man. She said all the right things and did all the right things to pump up my ego.

"She wasn't any prettier than your mama. She didn't have a better figure. She wasn't smarter, and she sure wasn't nicer than my Mary. She was just there telling me what I wanted to hear. Next thing I know I was off to Chicago with her.

"But it wasn't a party in Chicago. She had a new job waiting for her and lost it right away. And I couldn't find one. We both nearly starved trying to live. Romance went out the window then. It wasn't any fun at all then. We argued like crazy. We fought a few times, too. She started drinking like a fish. I didn't even want to be around her anymore.

"I wanted to go back with your mama. I wanted to go back with her so bad. I used to fantasize about being with Mary and you and Katherine again. They say you don't know what you have until it's gone. So true, that is. *So true.* But it was too late. When I called your mama and asked her if I could come back she told me to stay where I was. And then my friend Joe back in Jersey called me. He said he was dating her."

"What?" Jada shouted. "That is a lie! That man was always coming by to see Mama after you left, bringing her flowers and trying to take her out, but she wouldn't have anything to do with him. I saw her telling his butt off. Grandma and Katherine did too. It looks like you didn't have any decent friends either." Jada noticed that he didn't look surprised by her revelation. "Aren't you upset about this?"

"I learned that Joe lied a long time ago. He was dying of cancer and called me to his bed. He was confessing everything. He told me he lied about Mary being with him. He told me he wanted her, but she wouldn't have anything to do with him. He was sorry. But it was too late for me and your mama.

"I had spited her because I thought she was with him. I stopped sending things to you children because I knew it would hurt her. I stopped visiting you children because I knew that would hurt her, too. I stopped sending child support. I said she wasn't going to be looking good and eating good and being happy with my money while she slept with another man—and if it meant you children didn't get anything, you were just casualties of that war."

He sobbed heavily and his shoulders shook. "I'm so sorry, Jada. I was mad at her and didn't care about taking it out on you children. It wasn't right. I don't know what I was thinking. I am so, so sorry. I hate myself every day. And if you hated me, I would understand."

Jada wiped her teary eyes. "Why didn't you get in touch with us when you knew Mama hadn't done you wrong?"

He looked off sadly and began to rock. "Sometimes you drift so far away from people, you don't even know how to make your way back to them. I had done so much wrong, I just knew nobody would want to see me or talk to me, so I just let it go and missed ya'll so much. But I love you. I love you so much." He buried his face in his palms and cried.

Jada held on to him, her tears falling with his. By the time she left the chapel, they had decided to remain in each other's lives.

Outside the church, Jada embraced Randall and held him tightly.

He rubbed her back. "Baby, I hope this was a good thing I did getting you and your father together. I wanted him to tell you that he loved you. I didn't like you carrying that feeling around that he didn't. And I didn't want you to blame yourself for your parents' breakup."

She gazed up at him, cradling his face within her palms. "Yes, you did the right thing. No man has ever done something this nice for me. No one has ever cared and loved me like you do, Randall. Thank you so much."

"No, thank you, baby."

"For what?" she asked.

"For being in my life," he said, covering her mouth and pulling her close against his body.

Chapter Eighteen

Days after their return from North Carolina, Jada prepared for Gus's birthday party on his estate. She loved parties and always looked for a reason to get gussied up. Greatest of all, she looked forward to hearing good music and sampling the food.

She bought a new white jumpsuit for the party that molded to her figure perfectly. When Randall saw her sashay down her stairs into the living room where he waited for her, he grinned and shook his head. "Baby, you look beautiful. Just beautiful."

She checked him out in his white silk shirt with razor-sharp pressed jeans. "You're looking pretty good yourself, you beefcake." She patted him on his backside. "You have such a cute butt, Randall."

"I never thought of my butt as cute," he said humorously.

"That's because you're not a woman. We're experts on these things. If I got any group of women together and you walked by, you would definitely get a nod and more than that. Your booty is narrow and muscular and just so *cute*."

"If you say so," he said, laughing. "I'm just glad you like it. But if you want to know what I think about yours, I can show you better than I can tell you."

He came to her and kissed her deeply while gripping her backside and drawing her deep into him. "Ooh, baby," he groaned.

Once Jada felt his finger on the zipper of her outfit, she shoved him lightly. "Not now. We have a party to go to."

Randall sighed. "Oh, all right."

Jada wondered if the sigh was for her shunning their romantic rendezvous or something else. More than once, Randall expressed that he didn't want to see Linc at the party.

"Are you still thinking about Linc showing up?"

"He's going to show up all right. Gus would have a fit if he wasn't there."

"He would have a fit if you weren't there, too. Come on, baby. Get over this thing with Linc. You two might have to work together. You signed contracts and everything. But I know you don't want to talk about that. So let's get in our car and you can tell me what you're going to do to me later after we get home."

"Mmm, yummy," he said, ushering her out the door.

A half hour later, Jada strode along the lawn of Gus's huge estate. More than fifty guests scattered about the grounds and mansion. Eating, socializing, and dancing to jazz instrumentals and old pop standards, Jada had a great time.

Randall enjoyed himself also. He loved the band Gus had hired and didn't want to leave the entertainment when a young man whispered in his ear that Gus wanted to see him in his conference room. He pecked Jada on the cheek and promised to be right back.

Inside an upper room in Gus's mansion, Randall strode through double mahogany doors that led to Gus's meeting room. Once he entered it, he stopped short. Linc and Gus sat at the table.

"Sit down, son," Gus said to Randall, pulling out a chair that sat at the oblong wooden table.

Randall remained standing. "Gus, I know what you're trying to do. But he and I are not friends and I don't want to work with him. I thought you wanted to see me."

Gus walked over to Randall and put his arm around his shoulder. "I wanted to see both of you. I love both of you. That's why I went into the Sea Breeze Inn venture with both of you." He laid his hand against his heart. "But this war you two have is getting to be too much for me. I'm not a young man, Randall. I just want to make a little more money, a little profit with that hotel, so I can leave my family comfortable."

Randall eyed Gus warily. "Gus, are you sick?"

"Not really . . . my doctor has just told me that my heart has a minor problem."

Randall gasped.

Linc stood and walked over to Gus. He patted his back. "I'm sorry to hear that."

"Why didn't you tell us?" Randall asked.

Gus threw his hands in the air. "Look, the doctor said it's minor. I don't want to make a big deal of it. But if you two keep driving me crazy with this fighting, who knows what could happen to me?"

Randall disliked the emotional blackmail. At the same time, he would never do anything to jeopardize the health of his friend. "What can I do to help, Gus?"

"Me too?" Linc asked.

"You two can work things out and we can get this hotel up and running. Now talk and come out as partners." With that, Gus exited the room.

Through a strained silence, Randall narrowed his eyes at Linc. "I wish I never knew you."

Linc sighed. "Look. Let's just get everything off our chest now, so we can get past this. Is there anything you want to say to me?"

Randall grinned. "Say to you. No, I have nothing to say to you! I would just love to land my fist in your face one more time."

"You owed me one, so I let you get that off your chest that night at the club. But you put your hands on me again, Randall, and it's on."

Just then, a roar of laughter outside the door distracted them. Randall turned around and three guys came bursting into the room. Randall knew them from somewhere but didn't recall where until after a few seconds later. They were Linc's friends from the bar and grill.

"What you doing, man?" Ozzie asked Linc as the other two picked up knickknacks and examined them.

Randall frowned at the two with the sticky fingers.

"Just talking with my partner here," Linc responded. "Ya'll go out and I'll check you out downstairs. And I'm expecting your sister, Ozzie, my man."

"She's on her way," Ozzie replied and checked out the office on his way out. "Nice place. All the rooms are real nice. I think I'll give myself a tour of the upper floors."

"And I think you better not," Randall told him.

To that, Ozzie shot him a dirty look and strolled out the door with his two companions.

Linc leered at Randall. "What did you have to say that for? Why do you insult my friends, man?"

"Why did you bring those lowlifes here? You always get mixed up with the wrong type of people."

Linc frowned. "There you go again with your high and mighty lectures."

"You know I'm telling the truth. You always did hang around with the wrong type of people. Ever since I knew you, you always had to go hang with the so-called down people, trying to prove you weren't just some corny rich boy."

"You're just jealous because I had friends outside of you."

"Yes, you did. You had the kinds of friends who aren't really friends. The kind who have no goals and beg you to buy them drinks all the time, or loan them money. But *noooo*, good old Linc has to be down, so he has to give his friends what they want."

"I'm not going to apologize for not being uppity like you. Just because my dad made my life comfortable doesn't mean the only kind of people I hang around have to be rich like us."

"You're right. And I enjoy meeting all kinds of people, too. But I know what kind of people I'm not supposed to be around, and those guys that just left out of here are no good."

"Why? Because you say so?"

"Because I know so." He paused, hearing a noise. He assumed it to be Linc's friends hanging around and didn't care if they heard him. "I've seen them only twice and I know that they are no good. You know it, too."

"Randall, just stop messing with me. And stop being so angry. *She* doesn't stand between us anymore. Selena and I are over."

Randall heard another noise outside the door. He listened for more sounds for a moment and then concentrated again on Linc. "I am not angry about that anymore."

"You are! You're angry because I didn't just take any woman—I took your fiancée, the woman you were going to marry. But, man, how many times do I have to tell you I'm sorry? I regret doing it every day. I wish and wish I could take it back."

"I'm not mad about that! I have a woman. A wonderful, beautiful woman."

"You sure do," Linc agreed.

"And what the hell is that supposed to mean?"

"Damn, Randall, I'm just giving you a compliment and you can't even take it. Jada is beautiful, but I have no designs on her. All I'm thinking about these days is making money from the Sea Breeze Inn."

"It's done then! But only because of Gus, I'm going to work with you on this. Just don't expect me to like it and don't expect me to be friends with you. We're just business partners."

"Good. We can finally get things started."

With that, Linc left the room. With him gone, Randall immediately felt the air lighten for him. Then suddenly the door opened. Jada walked in with a strange expression.

"Hey, baby," Randall said. "What's wrong?"

"I was outside the door. I heard . . . I heard everything."

Randall swallowed. "Like what?"

"Like everything. You're so angry with Linc because he slept with your fiancée, Selena, and took her away from you. Randall, why didn't you tell me that's what Linc did to you? Here I am thinking it's about business or something far less important."

Randall looked away from her for a long while, before facing her again. "I didn't tell you because . . ."

"Because what?"

"Because it's so damn embarrassing! Who would want to tell his woman that his good friend and business partner took his ex? Sometimes now when I think about it, it sounds like it should be something that happened to somebody else, like it should be some gossip you hear about in passing. But it's not gossip. It's what happened in my life, Jada. I worked all the daytime, plus weeknights and weekends, and often traveled to St. Thomas building us a home, *and* her mother a house. Selena thought I was cheating instead of being a workaholic. And she turned to Linc."

Jada lowered her head in silence.

She remained quiet for so long that Randall asked, "What are you thinking?"

"Well, I'm thinking two things. One is that you should have trusted me and told me what happened. And two, you're *so* angry with him . . . you . . ."

"What?"

"You must still have feelings for her."

He grabbed her by the arms, forcing her to meet his gaze. "Oh, baby, no. Not now. I don't have feelings for Selena now. But I'll be honest. Even with her betraying me, there were some lingering emotions before you came. But since you've been in my life, you're all I think about. You're the only woman I want."

"Then why are you so angry with Linc?"

"*Because,*" he stated emphatically. "Linc was like one of my brothers. My brothers even thought of him as the sixth Larimore brother. He did things with our family. And because he had no siblings, he told us he felt we were like his brothers, too. And when your brother turns on you, it's the worst feeling in the world."

Jada didn't feel in the mood to party any longer. Randall and she wished Gus a happy birthday and left his estate early. Randall yearned to spend the night with her. Nevertheless, Jada claimed to be tired and wanted to go home and rest.

Rest eluded her. In her bed, she tossed and turned, thinking about this rage Randall felt toward Linc. Did he still harbor feelings for Selena? She pondered that question so much that she had a headache. Some time after, she fell asleep.

Hours later, Jada awakened in the middle of the night, feeling more refreshed. Her heart had also softened toward the matter with Randall and

Selena. Undoubtedly Randall loved her. He had proved it repeatedly, from the kind way he treated her, to reuniting her with her father. She had to hold on to that love and never doubt it.

Chapter Nineteen

Randall longed to give Jada something that truly expressed how much he treasured her being in his life. When he blindfolded her one afternoon and drove her downtown, he shared that he had a magnificent surprise for her.

He removed the blindfold at the Mercedes Benz car dealership. "Here we are."

Her eyes widened, Jada scanned the showroom decked with luxury coupes and vans. "Randall, you can't mean what I think you mean."

"But I do. Pick out any car you want."

"Randall, this is much too extravagant. There is a cute pair of sandals that I saw that you could treat me to if you just want to buy me something."

Randall laughed and pulled her to him by the waist. "You can have the sandals," he said, pinching her nose. "But I think you'll enjoy one of these babies much more." He laid his hand on the hood of a shiny green vehicle.

Jada whirled in disbelief. "Baby, you don't have to do this. I know you love me."

"And that is exactly why I'm doing it. I love you so much. What good is all this wealth I have if I can't spoil my queen?"

Jada hugged him, inhaling his sexy cologne and burying her cheek against his hard chest. "I love you, too. You have no idea how much."

Jada left the car dealership soaring on a high. She had ordered a candy-apple-red Mercedes Benz, complete with state-of-the art technology. Never had she owned a new car. Endlessly she kissed Randall for his generous gift. He promised more love presents. They headed downtown, where he treated her to lovely dresses, pants, blouses, skirts, shoes, bags, and jewelry from the finest boutiques. They also visited a bookstore and stocked up on the latest romance novel releases.

Famished from their all-day shopping spree, they strolled down the street in search of a fast-food restaurant. Jada turned into the doorstep of McDonald's when she noticed that Randall wasn't beside her. She swung around to see where he was.

He stood on the sidewalk, gazing across the street. Jada followed his line of vision to an attractive auburn-haired woman. She was rushing down the street, constantly looking back over her shoulder. Jada thought she behaved so peculiarly. She also wondered if Randall knew her.

A short distance from Jada, Randall had frozen. Yet how could he help it when he spotted Selena across the street? He assumed she had left the island since her breakup with Linc. It shocked him enough to see her again. It shocked him more to see how she behaved. The way her eyes darted over her shoulder repeatedly assured him that someone was following or chasing her. Several times he noticed her bumping into people in her hurry.

Then at one point, Randall spotted a man running in her direction. Selena sped off, nearly colliding with a car. The vehicle came to a screeching halt. Selena continued running until Randall no longer had her in sight. He lost sight of the man, too.

Jada tapped his shoulder. "Randall, do you know that woman who almost got hit by that car?"

"Uh, I noticed that she was running from something and I wanted to see what was going on."

Jada switched her gaze across the street to where the woman had nearly been struck by the car. "You think someone was after her? She was sure getting away from something, or someone."

"Yes, it seems that way," he said, putting his arms around Jada, walking toward the restaurant. "What about that grub we were going to get? My stomach is growling."

"Mine too, baby."

Later, after Jada and Randall had gone to her home and made love repeatedly, Jada woke up in the middle of the night. Lying beside Randall, hearing his soft breaths as he slept, she felt a fullness of love rising up in her chest. Even so, at the same time something in the back of her mind made her feel on edge.

She sat up, swung her shapely legs over the side of the bed, and walked over to the window. The moon was full. She wondered if it had anything to do with her mood. She felt restless. Then again, she knew it wasn't the moon. It was what had happened earlier in the day—Randall's stare at that mysterious woman.

She wasn't the jealous type. On the other hand, something about the scenario bothered her, mostly afterward. Randall had seemed distracted. At times, she felt as if she were talking to herself. She would ask him what she said, and he would apologize for being distracted about getting the Sea Breeze Inn up and running, along with the remainder of construction on the villas.

Why couldn't she believe him? It was just her old insecurities haunting her once again, she consoled herself. She had to forget it. This man loved her. She felt it. He showed it. God had finally sent her her dream and she just had to stop being fearful of losing him. She had to be grateful that they shared such a love. It was going to last forever.

Shortly after noon of the following day, Randall waited for an electrician inside one of his vacant villas. He inspected the room, sizing up what labor needed to be done and the cost. Passing a window, he came to a standstill, gazing out. Vivid daylight sparkling before him failed to keep his interest. Instead imagery from the previous day made him scowl. Selena was in some kind of trouble. But why did he care?

Certainly any love he harbored for her had died long ago. All the same, he hated for anything bad to happen to her. Murmurings around Lakeside had it that she and her family had parted ways. Perhaps that was why she hadn't returned home.

But possibly she believed Linc and she could get back together. Then again, he couldn't concern himself with them.

Life was so strange, he thought with a hint of a smile playing at the corners of his mouth. If Selena hadn't devastated him, he wouldn't have recaptured his love with Jada. For that alone he couldn't hold on to any grudges against Selena. He had reconnected with the love of his life, and the love was even greater than he ever imagined it would be, greater than what he had felt long ago for Selena. He loved Jada so much that lately he had passed jewelry store windows, gazing at their engagement rings. No harm in dreaming, he thought with a smile. Reuniting with Jada proved that dreams did come true.

Days later, Randall and Jada met Linc and Gus at the Sea Breeze Inn. Renovations were beginning and construction workers were scattered about the site. Jada did notice that Randall attempted to act more civilized with Linc as the three men went over the layouts. She saw Randall listening intently to Linc's very sharp ideas. She also observed Linc complimenting Randall repeatedly on his.

The only sore spot she saw between them were the three guys Linc had hired to work on the site. They were three of his friends, the same ones that she had run into at Gus's party. She found them fresh and vulgar. Now they did more beer drinking, eating, and resting than they did working.

At one point Jada went for a walk in the woods while Randall, Linc, and Gus inspected some of the rooms inside the hotel. That's when she saw the three men sitting with their backs against tree trunks, clowning around with each other. When she walked by them, they stood. Worse, they formed a circle around her. All had staid expressions on their faces.

"Should we let her go by, Ozzie?" one of them asked another.

Licking his two-toned lips, Ozzie looked thoroughly amused. "Maybe she doesn't really want to go by. Maybe she wants to hang out with us out here. You lonely, pretty lady?"

"No," Jada answered, "I would like to go back in the hotel." She made an attempt to walk by. One of the men jumped in front of her. The others laughed.

"You think that's funny?" Jada heard Randall say as he emerged in the wooded area.

He stepped close to the men. Instantly they unblocked Jada's path.

"What the hell do you think you're doing?" he asked, glaring at each of the three faces.

Ozzie grinned. "Man, we were just having a little fun. We always joke around. No harm done to your beautiful lady. No harm done."

"Your break is over," Randall said. "In fact, you're all fired."

"For what, man?" Ozzie spat. "For having some fun, lightening up the day?"

"It wasn't fun. You scared my woman. She didn't know what you were about to do to her. And neither do I." He slipped his arms around Jada's shoulders. "And I would kick your tail if you weren't employed by me!"

"Like the man said," a bald member of the trio added. "We meant her no harm."

"I don't believe that crap," Randall shot, and walked away holding Jada.

Two of the men also started back toward the hotel when they noticed Ozzie just standing, burning his gaze into Jada and Randall's back.

"That uppity rich boy needs to be taught a lesson," he uttered while grinding his teeth.

Chapter Twenty

When Randall reached the hotel, Linc stood outside talking to a worker. Randall approached Linc. Jada trailed him.

"I want those guys fired," he informed him.

Linc swiped the back of his hand over the sweat coating his face. "You want who fired?"

"Those friends of yours. I don't know why you hired them to work here in the first place. I bet you they are not qualified."

"They are. All are licensed contractors."

"Have you checked their references?"

"Of course. Randall, you know I don't play around with my business like that."

"I still want them fired. They encircled Jada over there in the woods and acted like they were going to do something to her. Who knows? They could have raped her."

Jada cringed at the thought.

"Randall, I wouldn't let them work here if they were dangerous. These men have children and families and need this work. They've been having problems getting work for a while." He eyed Jada. "Are you okay?"

Loathing the idea of robbing children of income, Jada nodded. More than anyone, she could relate to that. "I doubt they were going to hurt me. They were just kidding around."

Randall frowned at her. "Baby, don't stick up for them."

"I'm not. But please don't fire them. Just let's give them another chance."

"Why should we?" Randall asked.

"Because," she replied, "children might go hungry or homeless. I can't have that on my conscience and neither can you, Randall."

Squinting from the sun, Randall scoured the property. "Everything is going so smoothly. I would hate to screw it up because of a couple of bad apples. I'll give them one more chance."

Just then Gus called Randall inside, leaving Jada with Linc.

"You're a caring person, aren't you?" he said to her.

"I don't like kids missing a meal, if that's what you mean. Work can be hard to get sometimes. I was out of work in Jersey where I'm from and I looked and looked like crazy for a job, but nothing came about. Then Kelly told me about the job with the villas."

"Randall is lucky. Lucky that you came to work with him and lucky that you're his woman. And I mean no disrespect."

She smiled. "I know you mean no harm. Can I help you with anything? I feel so useless seeing you guys doing everything."

Linc thought for a moment. "You know, you can help me with something. Randall told Gus and me that you might want to paint, and I was going to start that in the upper rooms. Maybe you can help me?"

"Paint," she said in a joking voice. "Man, I was born for painting."

Linc chuckled and led the way. For hours they painted the upstairs room, getting acquainted as they did so. He shared that he was an only child and talked about his career. He also told her funny stories about Randall and his first experiences in business. He enjoyed hearing things about her life as well.

By the time they had finished painting one room, he felt that he had known Jada much longer than he had. He also kept telling himself that she was Randall's woman. Maybe that would stop the desire that welled up in him each time he looked at her.

Linc returned to his boat that evening. Quickly he showered, preparing for a date. Gabriella, Ozzie's Afro-wearing younger sister, had been his companion often after his split-up with Selena. Many hot-blooded nights they shared. Linc didn't consider their pairing serious. Gabriella agreed with his sentiment. They regarded themselves as two adults, simply enjoying each other's company with no strings attached and no commitments.

Within minutes after Gabriella's arrival on the boat, Linc's well-built body tangled with her athletic one among blue satin sheets. Like a madman, he pumped her, thrashing his hips into a frenzied pace with hers. He delighted in all the honey that she beguiled him with and groaned from the extreme joy.

Gabriella cried with ecstasy and screamed so loudly that anyone passing by the docked cruiser could have heard them. Hearing her sexy sounds, Linc felt his sexual appetite heightened. His eyes shut tight. Suddenly Gabriella vanished. Another woman lay writhing beneath him, her body wet from the satisfaction he bestowed her with. He thrust deeper inside her and kissed her equally as potently, his mouth and his erection thrilling her. Rapture became too much for him to repress or hang on to.

Uncontrollably Linc shook, embracing her tighter, kissing her deeper, loving her harder. "Jada, you make it so good, baby. Jada, oh, Jada, Jada, Jada."

"Who is she?"

Striving to catch his breath, Linc opened his eyes. Gabriella, her face shining from their passionate episode, was livid.

"She's nobody. I apologize."

Gabriella sat up, covering her breasts and below with the sheet. "Don't lie to me, man."

"I told you I apologize. And she is nobody for you to concern yourself with."

"I hate a lying man."

"And I hate a woman who says she is okay with just keeping things light and kicking it when she's really scheming to have a committed relationship." He snatched his shorts up from the floor and stepped into them. "I told you I didn't want to become seriously involved with you and you said you were okay with that, because that's what you wanted, too." He picked up his slacks and stepped into them, too.

"Yes, I said that, but what I feel for you has changed my mind."

"So what are you saying?" he asked, but he already deciphered her meaning from her expression.

"I want more than giving it to you all night, Linc. I want you to be my man and act like my man. And I want you to forget this woman. Have you been sleeping with her? Have you brought her to the boat and made love to her in this same bed where you made love to me? The thought of that unnerves me."

"That's really none of your business."

"When you're tapping this," she said with a smack of her backside, "it is my business."

Linc chuckled, but one glance at her fuming face calmed him down. "No, all right? I haven't slept with her. She's just someone I know."

"And you want her body?"

Linc half smiled, half frowned at the absurdity of the question. Why did he have to get involved with one of his friend's sisters anyway? He never became involved with his buddies' sisters. Partners cringed at the thought of becoming mixed up with each other's close blood. Without uttering the words, they were always off-limits.

Oddly enough, Ozzie had encouraged Linc to date his younger sister, twenty-nine-year-old Gabriella. But Linc wasn't a fool. Ozzie talked about money so much, anyone knew he had an unwholesome love affair with it. From Linc's viewpoint, Ozzie presumed that if he hooked up with Gabriella and things did become serious, the money would be all in the family. In any case, he remained around Ozzie, because he rationalized that everyone had faults, especially himself. Still, sometimes what Randall said about his choice of friends did cross his mind.

"What do you want from me, Gabriella? What do you really want? Why are you with me?"

"Answer my question, Linc. Don't try to get out of it by interrogating me. I want us to be honest and open."

"Do you really want that? Because I've been honest with you since I met you. Have you been honest with me? Like have you been dating me because of my fat bankroll?"

She reared back. "You have some nerve. You think I lie on my back with you because of money?"

"I had to ask it."

"No, no, no. You're just trying to get out of answering me. But you're not. Do you want her body?"

"What do you think?"

"You're fantasizing about her when you're making love to me. You're pretending she's the one you're making love to. I'll forgive you this one time. But I want you to stop it. I don't ever want to hear her name again, or I'm gone."

"Tell me one thing though. How do I stop myself?" He knew this would enrage her and that's what he wanted. She had irritated him so much he wanted her gone.

"What?"

"You heard me. How do I stop myself from calling out a woman's name because she's on my mind? How do I stop thinking and wanting and needing her? How do I stop myself from feeling something, no matter how much I don't want to? I just can't stop thinking about her or wanting her. She's all I think about."

Gabriella's light brown skin reddened. "You disrespect me like this?"

"You asked for the truth."

"Screw you, man," she shot, grabbing her clothes from different areas of the room. "Wait until I tell Ozzie how you spit on my heart."

"I'm sorry, Gabriella. But we said we weren't going to get serious. Now you're flipping the script on me. Or is it all part of the game to get your hands on my money?"

"Money, my behind! Man, I work. My physical therapy position pays me just fine. I wanted to be with your sorry behind because I have feelings for you. I thought you were feeling the same thing, too. But nooooo. You think because you're some rich guy from some fancy family that I'm not good enough."

"I never said that."

"Your actions tell the truth. I'm just good enough for the action in the dark, but not good enough for nothing else. I know this woman is probably some educated, fancy woman who you would love to take around your family. She's probably rich, too. You don't have to worry about her taking from you."

"All I want to know is why you're tripping after we said we weren't going to get serious."

"Why do you think, man? How would you feel if a woman called another man's name when you're giving her all the loving you got?"

The question brought him to a place he didn't want to go. Selena had called him Randall once. "Leave then."

"Not before I say my piece. Man, don't you know women? Don't you know what it means when we give a man our bodies? You give him a piece of your soul and that means something. But you'll see the consequences of what you've done. I'm going to tell Ozzie how you disrespected me. *Beware.*"

Gabriella dressed in silence. Her *beware* lingered with an eerie noiselessness in the room. But what did he have to fear? Ozzie was his buddy. He understood male and female entanglements. Sometimes things didn't work out. Sometimes lovers even became enemies.

Overall, he recognized tonight that he shouldn't have become involved with her. Women that pretended not to care when they really did were the most possessive kind. How many stories had he heard from his buddies about a woman that was a casual sex partner, who had slit a man's tires or busted the windows of his Lexus? Occasionally they even stalked a guy when he dated another woman. He didn't need that from Gabriella.

Besides, she wasn't the type of woman he wanted to get involved with. They had nothing in common. While he loved to talk about the finer things in life, she loved to talk about the island rumors. Their highest connection had been sex—which he had to admit was good—but not that good for her to get on his nerves like she did tonight.

He thought of her a few more moments and also wondered what he would say to Ozzie the next time he saw him. Then he thought of whom he always thought of when he was alone lately—Jada. He couldn't even control himself from calling out her name when making love to Gabriella. She had gotten to him that deeply. What was he going to do?

With every second spent around Jada, he became more enamored by her. It was a feeling stronger than he ever had for Selena. It was to the point where he had to remind himself what was important: his relationship to Randall.

Yes, he wanted Jada so much that he could hardly stand it. But if he stayed strong and controlled himself, the feeling would disappear. It had to. Randall was his friend unlike any other, the kind of friend that came along once in a lifetime. He doubted he was ready to give up another woman to him. So he would love Jada the only way he could. Linc sprawled across his bed. Folding his hands behind his head, he closed his eyes tight. He sucked in a breath as he undressed her and they made love in his mind.

Outside, Gabriella strode along the pier slowly. She had become so enraged by Linc's treatment that she couldn't remember where she had parked her car. Finally, she stopped and just stood. She tried to recall where she had parked, but her misery consumed her.

Yes, when Ozzie first told her about Linc, both of them were especially interested in his money. But when she met Linc and became involved with him, she cared less about snagging a rich man. Linc was one of the handsomest men she had ever met. He was classy and acted as if he owned the world. She adored him. And when they at last made love, he had been such an expert lover that she fell deeper under his spell.

Sure, she told him that she longed for nothing serious like he did. But how else could she hold on to his love and make him hang around long enough to fall in love with her? Now her dream was gone. Her plan had backfired. Her heart was crumbling.

But Linc could not destroy her this way and expect to have peace. She would see to that. Then Ozzie would take care of him. If one person loved her in this world, it was her brother.

Chapter Twenty-one

Early the next morning when Jada awakened in Randall's bed, he thrilled her with hot lovemaking. In the after silence that succeeded their sultry moment, she wondered aloud, "This is just too good to be true."

He nestled her close to him, coaxing her head on his chest. "Well, it's true, my love. Everything is perfect in our lives right now. You've been talking to your dad again. Everything is great with my family right now. Everything is great with yours. Business is booming. The hotel is even going to be ready sooner than planned. But most of all, I have you in my life again." He pecked her on the lips and then squeezed her in his arms, kissing her lingeringly.

When they uncoupled, she laughed. "We better get to work."

"Is working at both sites too much for you? Because you really don't have to come to the inn, baby."

"I like going there. It's been fun. And I'm happy to see you and Linc getting along."

"I'm just trying to keep the peace for Gus's sake. Plus, the inn is going to be a big moneymaker." He swung his legs over the side of the bed. "I'm going to take a shower. Want to join me?"

"In a minute." Glowing, she watched him strutting into the bathroom and was tempted to pinch his butt. He was so gorgeous. More importantly, he was so sweet. After a while of lazing among the covers, she did force herself up. She needed a towel for after her shower and couldn't remember which closet Randall kept his towels in.

She yelled to Randall in the bathroom, asking him. However, the shower stream poured so loudly that he couldn't hear her. Hence, she peeked in several of his many closets, searching for the linens. One closet she peeked in, she saw photo albums.

Curious, she removed one and scanned through the pages. She saw numerous pictures of Randall's family, and then one of a woman with Randall. She looked so familiar, Jada tried to figure out where she had seen her. Then it came to her.

Randall, wondering what took Jada so long, walked out of the shower with a towel wrapped around his bottom. "What's taking you so long? Your baby is in need."

Jada felt her heart racing. "You lied to me."

"What are you talking about?"

"That woman. The one we saw running. You do know her. She's right here in your photo album. Is she Selena?"

With a sigh, Randall nodded. "Yes."

"Why wouldn't you tell me it was her?"

"Because I didn't want any problems, Jada. Look at how you're acting now. What did I do anyway? I just saw her running like someone was chasing her and I wanted to see what was going on. I made no attempt to talk to the woman. I have no intentions of talking to or seeing the woman. She's out of my life. You're in my life. You're the one I want to be with forever."

Jada sighed. "I just don't understand why you didn't tell me it was her. It makes me feel weird. What is she doing here anyway? She's no longer with Linc."

"Baby, I have no idea why she is here. And I don't care. All I care about is you. Now can you please come to the shower and give your man all that good loving that he's so hungry for and not let this woman spoil our day?"

Jada softened with his sexy plea and the corners of her lips inched up in a smile. "I'm coming."

At the hotel site, Linc didn't know what to expect from Ozzie. Oddly enough, his buddy never mentioned Gabriella, or Linc's tiff with her. In fact, Linc was elated that Ozzie seemed to work harder than he ever had. He was also grateful to paint another room with Jada. Again, they became more acquainted. Again, he had to remind himself that she was Randall's woman.

On the site grounds, Randall toiled equally hard. He supervised construction. As well, he performed hands-on work with the restoration as much as he could. Resentment still lingered toward Linc, though he tried his hardest to be civilized.

Nonetheless, he couldn't hide his distrust and dislike for Linc's friends. Often he noticed the men cornered off talking and watching Gus and him with angry eyes. Randall especially noticed how they would smile in Linc's face and their smiles would fade once Linc walked by.

Over and over he told Linc that he didn't trust Ozzie and his crew. Linc still insisted that they were his good friends, that he still felt the same way about Randall, too—like a brother.

Randall hardly shared that sentiment. That's why he secretly observed his behavior around Jada. Linc gave an Oscar-winning performance of trying to hide it. Yet Randall knew him and knew that he desired his woman. No way in the world that fantasy would come true. This was the woman that he truly, truly loved.

Weeks flew by. The hotel began to take up so much of Jada and Randall's time that their workload at the villas had backed up. One day at dusk, when Jada entered his office after sorting through a batch of paperwork, she rotated her shoulders, trying to rid them of stiffness.

Randall saw her attempt to loosen up as a cry for a massage.

"Oh, that feels wonderful," she said, soon feeling his fingers working through the impressions along her shoulders and up the small of her back. Sitting on an uncluttered portion of his desk while he stood behind her, she shifted to grant him a better angle for his sweet handling. "You sure can do that good."

"I can do a lot of things good," he said huskily and came around to the front of her.

Tenderly he kissed her lips and felt her hands rising to his shoulders. He pulled her to the edge of the desk. Then he glided into the space between her legs, drawing her close to him by the waist. His excitement reached a fever pitch by the time he eased everything off the remainder of the desk and laid her back on it.

While her legs dangled over the edge, Randall bent down and sprinkled kisses on them, before massaging them erotically. When he reached her thighs, he shoved up her skirt and caressed her soft warmth. She squirmed and writhed, forcing him to slide her skirt off and then her panties.

So heated he couldn't stand it, he shed his own clothing and then removed the remainder of hers. After protecting them, he pulled her womanhood closer to the corner and edge of the desk. With one light push, he eased inside her.

Jada lay back on the desk feeling as if she were climbing the walls. The ecstasy became too intense. At one point, she held on to Randall. At another point, she screamed out and held herself. Then in one earth-shattering moment, their orgasmic pleasure was reached much too soon.

Exhausted and thoroughly satisfied from lovemaking with Jada, Randall desired to hold her, to sleep and wake up to thrill her sexy body again. Unfortunately, though, he had scheduled a meeting with a banker at a local gentlemen's club.

Moments later, he maneuvered through downtown Charlotte Amalie until traffic forced him into a standstill. Bouncing his head to R. Kelly's song "Stop in the Name of Love" playing on the radio, he thought about Jada. Naughty recollections of her transforming his office into an erotic playground gave him a huge grin. He couldn't wait to get back to her, and honked his horn.

As he glanced sideways out the window, a sight made him do a double take. His mouth uncurled once he spotted Selena. Hurriedly she was walking down the street in an obvious disguise. Even with her wearing dark shades and covering her auburn locks with a long black wig, he knew her face anywhere.

As soon as traffic permitted, Randall wheeled his car in her direction. He parked it and approached her from behind.

"Selena?"

Her head snapped around at the familiar voice. "Randall, you recognize me?"

"Why wouldn't I?"

"That's bad." She looked around nervously. "That's really bad."

"What's going on, Selena?"

"Randall, I'm in trouble. I'm in the biggest trouble of my life."

"I know something is happening with you. I saw you nearly get hit by a car one day because you were running so fast. What's up?"

Carefully she scanned the area again and then gaped at him. "Help me. Please help me. I know I did you wrong, but I know you wouldn't want to see me dead."

He frowned. "Woman, what is going on with you?"

"I can't tell you here."

Randall hated the thought of missing an important business meeting. Yet if he let something happen to Selena, it would bother him forever. He took out his cell phone and called the banker. They decided to reschedule the meeting. Shortly after, he escorted Selena to his Mercedes Benz.

He drove her to a secluded area by a lake. "So what is going on?" he asked, turning off the car ignition.

"Someone is trying to kill me," she sobbed.

He gawked at her in disbelief. "Why in the world would someone try to kill you?"

"Because I saw something."

"Something like what?"

"A man getting killed."

"You saw someone getting killed?"

"It's true, Randall. I saw a man getting killed and the killers saw me."

He considered what she said for several seconds. "Have you gone to the police?"

"I'm too scared."

"You have to go to the police, Selena. You don't want to run forever."

"I'm scared, Randall. I'm scared to death."

"How did they kill the man?"

"It was three of them. They beat him. They shot him. Then they threw him in the ocean."

Randall studied her quietly. He knew she definitely ran from someone, but he had to wonder if this story was the truth. What if she had done something to make someone come after her? "Don't play with my head. I missed an important meeting to listen to you."

"Randall, I'm telling you the truth. The day after I witnessed the murder, I saw a picture of the man in the paper. They described him as a missing person. Days later, they said they had found his body. He's some politician. He was supposed to have done a lot of good things for people."

"Then you need to give a good man some justice and tell the police."

Wildly she shook her head. "Randall, I can't. You know what happens to snitches. They are permanently silenced."

"So you're going to keep running like this?"

"I need to get off this island."

"So why can't you go?"

"I tried to do that once, and while I was at the airport they spotted me. I ran for my life. I had to run so fast and duck into all kinds of places to get away from them."

"How did this all happen? How did you of all people happen to see a murder?"

"I was going to Linc's place around three in the morning." She hesitated. "I was feeling lonely after he and I broke up. The guys hurting this guy thought no one was around. But I spotted them. I saw what they did. It was so awful. I couldn't believe it. I have never seen anyone get killed before. They wouldn't even have seen me if I hadn't dropped my purse on the dock and made a noise."

"Have you told Linc?"

She hesitated in answering. Linc's friends were the killers. She believed Linc had nothing to do with it. Yet if she identified them to Randall and Linc, all of them could be endangered.

"He changed his number after we broke up, so he wouldn't have to talk to me. I can't get the new one. And I can't go to his boat. They might see me. They are . . . they are in that vicinity a lot. When you see me out and about, it's only because I'm trying to get food and little things I need. I stay at this little hotel. Randall, what am I going to do? Can you help me? Doesn't Hunter have a plane that he can fly down here and fly me out?"

Randall took a deep breath, pondering her dilemma. One part of him wanted to help her. The other part warned him to stay out of it. After all, look at the devastation she had caused him. "You need to talk to Linc. He brought you here. And he should be the one to help you. He's working on a hotel with me. You can come by if you want to take a chance. I'll give you directions."

"You're working with Linc? You're friends again?"

"No, we're not friends. But we bought that inn together and I'm sure enough going to make a profit of it."

"I read about it in the paper. I hear that you're going to have a big grand-opening party for it. I wish I could come. I wish my life was simple again and fun. I've lost everything and now I might even lose my life."

"Stop talking like that. And why can't you call your family to come down here and help you get out?"

"My family hates me."

"Why do you say that?"

"Because I alienated them. I did that to everybody. Snubbed them when I was riding high with you, and then with Linc. I bragged about being with rich men and didn't give a darn about any of them, didn't visit them, didn't call, didn't care if someone was sick and just wanted me to stop by and see them and let them know I cared.

"So when I needed them, nobody cared. I called them about this situation and they told me to go to the police. I've been living in a motel off of some money Linc gave me. But it's running out. Everything is running out. My life is running out. But, Randall, you have to help me. There is no one else."

"Linc is the person who should help you. You came here with him."

She shook her head. "I don't even know if he would help me if I saw him. He doesn't love me anymore. He hates me."

"And why is that?"

She looked off in the distance silently.

"Guess that's none of my business," Randall responded to her hush.

"I just don't want to get into that now. But I want to thank you, Randall. I was so happy to see you. You were like an angel that just came out of nowhere when I needed you. But you were always that way to me."

"I just happened to be at that spot and saw you."

"No, it was more than that, Randall. It was like fate brought us back together. I knew you were coming down to move into that house you bought us and to see about your villas, but I had no idea you had arrived yet. I've been here all this time and never ran into you. But now that I have, I want us to stay in each other's lives. I need you to help me through this, Randall. I have no one else."

At 10:45 P.M. Randall returned home stressed. Selena's dilemma scrambled through his head and he regretted ever approaching her. The phone ringing tugged him out of his musings.

He reached across his bed to the end table, picking up the receiver. "Hello."

"Randall, where have you been?" Jada asked.

"Hello to you, too, Ms. Gracen." His tenseness

waned at hearing her voice. He relaxed back on his bed, dropping his head onto a pillow.

"Baby, I was worried about you. The banker called the office when you didn't show up."

"Oh, I called him. We rescheduled already."

Silence hung between them. He debated telling Jada about Selena.

"So aren't you going to tell me?"

"Tell you what, beautiful?"

"Randall, where were you all that time? What caused you to miss such an important meeting?"

In light of their past with a former lover breaking them up, Randall knew the truth would cause all hell to break loose. "I ran into a friend who had some problems with various things and he needed to talk. He was in bad shape."

"Is he okay now?"

"Yes, much better."

"You always make people feel better."

"I try. But I want to forget all that. Talk sexy to me. Or just tell me why you're crazy about me."

Jada giggled. "That list is so long."

"Come with it, baby." He rose up from the mattress, sliding his slacks down his legs.

"Well, I think you're wonderful. You're a *good* man. You have a good heart."

"And what else do I have that's good to you?"

"Um," Jada purred. "You have something so good that it makes me smile way deep down inside."

"Oh yes, big daddy knows what to do to make you smile. But how can I help it when I have a wonderful hot mama like you to endow with my natural gift?"

"You sure have a *superior* natural gift," she whispered.

"And you have superior everything. You're beautiful." His voice was laden with huskiness.

"Umm, tell me more."

"You have the sexiest eyes a man would ever want to look into."

"Go on."

"And your lips." He groaned. "Those lips can drive a man crazy."

"Only want to drive one man crazy with them. But tell me more."

"Oh, and that soft, satiny skin. I just want to lie against you all the time and rub my . . ." He laughed lowly and heard her laugh with him. "And kiss every sweet inch."

"I wish you were here kissing every inch right now."

"And then there's that body. Lord, have mercy!"

"You like my body?" she purred again.

"Like it," he echoed. "Woman, there's no like in it. I live for it. I love those big pretty legs and those big juicy thighs. Wish I could bury my face into them right now."

"You're fresh, Randall. Tell me more freshness."

"Oh, there is plenty to tell. Moving right along, I'm a brother and I started loving booty from my crib."

Jada laughed loudly.

"So when I saw yours, you know I lost my mind. You have the prettiest, roundest one that I have ever seen. Ooh, and when you're naked." He groaned. "Oh my *God*, I just love to squeeze and kiss it, and I love to do each real, real slow."

"Randall, some would call you a freak."

"And what do you call me, baby?"

"Umm, I'm calling you over here right now. I'm

overdue for some of the good loving that only you can give."

"I'm leaving the house right now. Keep it hot for me, baby."

Chapter Twenty-two

One early afternoon when Randall arrived at the Sea Breeze Inn, he was grateful that everything was moving along smoothly. After all, they were days from their grand opening gala. Construction proceeded with all of the workers putting forth their greatest effort on their individual projects. Meanwhile Gus sat a table in a discussion with an architect. Jada chatted with an interior designer. The only people that Randall couldn't account for were Linc and his three rowdy buddies.

In search of the missing foursome, he trampled through the woods, their usual hiding spot. He spotted Linc sitting on the ground with his friends. Beer cans scattered around them. Randall ducked out of sight behind some bushes because he was curious what they talked about.

"Gus is such an upstanding guy," Linc said, "that he found money in one of the rooms of this place when we first bought it and called the authorities to see if anyone claimed it. When no one did after a certain amount of time, the authorities gave the money back to Gus. And you know he put it right back in the place where the person had hid it. He thinks they might come back for it. That's what an upstanding guy Gus is."

"Well, if he don't want it, I'll take care of it," Ozzie said jokingly. "Which room is it in anyway and hidden where?"

"No, man. Let him leave it where it is. Don't worry anyway. You're going to have plenty of money for your family. I can hook you up here at the hotel to do all kinds of work. You always tell me you're a jack of all trades."

"That's cool," Ozzie said, "but, man, why let that money just rot somewhere in a room?"

"Drop it, man," Linc said with a laugh, but he saw that his buddy wasn't amused.

"Why should I? Only a fool would let free money go to waste."

"Come on, Ozzie. Gus is an old man. Let him do what he wants."

"While money just hides in a room somewhere," Ozzie declared.

"Drop it, man," Linc insisted, surprised at Ozzie's growing anger over this. "Ease up. It's not his money, mine, or *yours*, so we shouldn't worry about it."

Ozzie hopped to his feet. "You don't tell me what to worry about when you owe me so much. I gave you something precious."

"What are you talking about?"

"You know what I'm talking about!"

Linc frowned. "You're talking about Gabriella?"

"I gave you my sister and you spit on her heart."

"Look, man, I'm sorry about all that. I'm sorry

about this disagreement we're having too. I didn't expect for a little talk about some money to come down to this. But if you don't want to work here anymore, I'll be glad to give you your pay right now."

Ozzie peered at him for a long while and then suddenly burst out laughing. "Got you. I got you good, didn't I? You thought I was mad."

Linc exhaled his relief and laughed. "You sure did. I thought you were pissed at me."

"Just kidding, man. And that thing with you and Gabriella, that's your business. I stay out of my family's love affairs and they stay out of mine. And I don't care about the money hidden in the hotel either. I know you're going to hook me up." He put his arm around Linc and patted his shoulder.

"I always hook up my partners," Linc boasted.

Randall stepped from behind the bushes and headed toward the group of men. Like fleeing insects, Ozzie and his two companions left, heading back to the hotel.

Randall blocked Linc's path, so he couldn't join them. "Are you crazy?"

"What are you bugging me about now, Randall?"

"You're here telling those no-good guys Gus's business. Why did you tell them about the money Gus found? What is wrong with you? You hang out with the wrong people and you talk too damn much to them. One of these days it's all going to get you in trouble. You mark my words."

Randall stomped off away from him and toward the hotel.

Linc sat on the ground, thinking about what

Randall said. Deep down, he knew that Ozzie and his gang weren't the most upstanding men. In the past few days, he had even uncovered that Ozzie had once committed armed robbery.

Yet Ozzie and the rest treated him like one of them. Ozzie liked him so much that he hadn't even cared about his treatment of Gabriella. And he craved that acceptance.

Growing up he was always the rich kid, the one on the outside looking in. Most of the people he knew didn't have what he had. He was thinking about all this when he noticed Jada strolling through the woods, picking fruit from the trees.

Deciding to have some fun and scare her, he hid back behind some bushes. When she approached him, he jumped out. "Boo!"

Jada was so startled she stumbled back. He tried to break her fall and fell on top of her. Linc couldn't move right away. Lying on top of her soft, succulent body, he lost himself in her sexy eyes; that is, until he heard the rustle of approaching footsteps.

Randall soon stood above them. He reached his hand down to Jada.

Getting on her feet, she hoped he didn't jump to the wrong conclusion. "Baby, I was falling and Linc tried to break it and fell on top of me."

"I'm clumsy," Linc told her and Randall.

Randall narrowed his eyes at Linc. "Don't play games with me, man. I know you."

"I'm not playing anything," Linc responded. "Of course I can't help but notice that Jada is a beautiful, sexy woman. But she's your woman, and I respect that and would never do anything to interfere with it."

With that, Linc walked off.

Randall plopped onto the ground, looking infuriated.

"Baby, he didn't do anything. And you trust me, don't you?" She kissed him.

Kissing her back, he drew her close. "Yes, I trust you. I just will never trust *him*."

The day before the grand opening of the hotel, Jada and Randall felt they deserved a day off. After all, a monumental project had been completed. They wanted to spend time alone, doing things that they enjoyed. Their first fun spot was an out-of-the-way bookstore that sat at the end of Valeria Beach. As Jada strode among the thousands of books and paneled walls, complemented by rich cherry-wood bookcases and hardwood floors, she thought of her long-ago dream.

Randall saw that dreamy look in her eye. "You just can't shake that idea of owning your own bookstore, can you?"

"It's hard to get rid of your dreams. But I'm saving my pennies."

"Oh, you are?" he teased, following her through the rows as she read the spines of various books.

"I like the idea of bookstores like this, at out-of-the-way places. If this were my store, I would have romances of course, lots of suspense, mysteries, self-help, Christian books, and all sorts of stuff. I would have comfortable wooden tables and chairs for people to read and a place in the store for signings. I would send out mailings to all the townspeople and try to have a new writer there every Friday or Saturday night. Give people something to look forward to."

"That sounds beautiful, baby. You're beautiful." They kissed long and languidly until a toddler passed staring at them. After Jada walked out of the store with tons of new books, Randall lingered behind for a few moments checking the store out. He wanted to be Jada's genie and make her every wish come true. He had a few surprises up his sleeve.

Later that day, Jada and Randall kicked back at her house watching videos and eating popcorn and pretzels. They enjoyed movies like *Cooley High, Love and Basketball, The Best Man, Set it Off,* and *What Lies Beneath.* Then they watched another release, *Unfaithful.* In the midst of the last movie they watched before turning in, Randall's cell phone rang. He ignored it for several moments before answering. His answers to the other party were so cut-and-dry that Jada couldn't help but ask who it was when he hung up.

"There's a problem with one of the villas. I have to take care of it."

"Right now?" Jada asked testily.

"It's urgent, baby." He pecked her on the cheek. "I'll call you when I come back."

Jada noticed that he couldn't even look her in the eyes when he spoke to her. It all gave her the strangest feeling—a feeling that made her get in her car and follow him.

When he finally pulled into a parking lot, Jada's heartbeat froze and then beat much too fast. Randall was at a motel.

Jada's ears and head started to beat in a frenzied pace just like her heart. After Randall entered the motel, she waited a while before she entered it, too.

"What room did that man that just came in here go to?" she asked the blue-eyed man behind the counter.

"Lady, I respect people's privacy."

Jada reached in her purse and put a fifty-dollar bill on the counter.

"I just lost some respect," the man said, tucking the bill in his shirt pocket. "That guest's name would be Selena Mason."

Chapter Twenty-three

As Randall strode inside Selena's room, he was surprised she stayed there. The other day he had only dropped her in front of the motel, so he had no idea how the inside looked. Compared to the lavish lifestyle that he was accustomed to seeing her in, he knew it must have been an adjustment for her to live so modestly. She sprawled across the bed, crying. He pulled up a chair next to her bed.

"Randall, thank you for coming to see me." She patted his hand. "And thank you for listening to me the other day and driving me away to safety."

"Whatever happened between us, I don't want to see you in trouble, Selena. Now what is this emergency you summoned me here for?"

"I'm out of money. The motel says that this is my last day. I feel so desperate, Randall. Can you help me? If you arranged for me to get off the island, it would save my life. I know it would."

"I told you to go to the police, and I told you to go to Linc. Why don't you call him to help you?"

"And I told you he hates me."

"Why does he hate you? What happened?" She clammed up again, so he added, "He should be the one helping you get off the island. I did not bring you here. We are not part of each other's lives anymore. So why should I be responsible?"

She nodded. "You're right. But there is something I didn't tell you."

"What?"

"Linc knows the killers."

"What?"

"They're friends of his. It could get us all in a lot of trouble."

Randall thought for a moment. "You're not talking about Ozzie and those two goons that he hangs out with, are you?"

She knew if she told Randall the truth, he would go to the police and also involve Linc. She couldn't endanger any of them. "No way, not Ozzie. I know the guys by face, but I don't know their names."

Randall studied her. "Are you sure it's not Ozzie? Because I have met that character and I know he's crooked."

"No, it's not him," she lied.

Randall stood. "Look, Selena, I tried to help you, but all I can do is tell you to go to the police or Linc. I can't do any more. You can even see Linc at the party tomorrow for the opening of the hotel if you want to catch him. There will be lots of people there, the press and everything. So there will be less of a chance for anyone to hurt you. Besides, we will have high security."

"I'm still scared."

"Well, I can't help you anymore."

"Wait." She grabbed his arm as he tried to walk away.

"What do you want now?"

"To talk about us."

Randall took a deep breath. "This is very awkward."

"Randall, I understand your reluctance. After all, what I did to you was horrible. It's unforgivable. But I've changed."

"I'm glad you've changed. We all need to grow and move forward."

"Can we move forward?"

Randall's eyes crinkled as he tried to absorb her meaning.

"I mean, can you and I have another chance? Randall, I never stopped loving you. I told you before that I slept with Linc because I truly believed you were cheating on me instead of working all the time like you actually were."

"But you're forgetting one fact here, Selena. After you told me all this and I said no, you went right back to Linc. Shucks, you two started living together. Even came down here to the island together. Now, what kind of love do you feel for me when you do that? I don't get that part."

"I just needed someone. You kicked me out of your life. I had to have someone and he was already there."

"I'm sorry. It all just sounds like words. He doesn't want you, so now you're running back to me. But you're wasting your breath. We could never be together again."

Selena began to sob. "You keep asking why Linc hates me. It's you, Randall. He hates me because of you."

"What are you talking about?"

"Because he hates that I never fell in love with him and always wanted you back. More than once when we made love, I screamed out your name. I even mumbled it in my dreams. He couldn't take it anymore. He said he couldn't make me happy, because I still loved you and I had never loved him. I confessed that it was true.

"You can ask him if you don't believe me. He cursed me out and told me he had lost the best friend he ever had because of me, and I didn't even care about him. And I did care. I just didn't love him. I still love you, Randall. Is there a chance for us? I still see something in your eyes. Something that tells me you're still in love with me."

Jada had wandered around the streets aimlessly when she noticed men were watching her. Men that looked like they were up to no good. She started toward her car, but realized that she didn't feel like driving. She couldn't concentrate. She hailed a cab.

The taxi driver asked Jada her destination. So dazed was she that he had already started driving before she registered his question and answered, "I'll let you know where to take me. Just drive."

He drove up the road and to downtown. Among the places that they passed, she saw a bar. She wasn't a drinker, but some said drinking eased the pain away.

"Here," she said, pointing to Sonny's Bar and Grill. "I'll get out here."

After shelling out several dollars to the driver, Jada sauntered in the bar's direction. Patrons scattered about the outside of the nightspot socializing. Numerous men tried to strike up a conversation with her as she made her way to the mahogany door. One touched her arm. Barely aware of anyone, Jada acted unresponsive. She walked inside Sonny's and took a seat at the counter.

"What are you doing drinking alone, pretty lady? What are you having tonight?" The dreadlocked bartender greeted her in a mellifluous island accent and a piano-white smile.

Jada mulled over what to drink, but became distracted when the bartender's eyes floated over her shoulder. She made a motion to swing around when Linc slid onto the bar stool next to hers.

"This is one of my hangouts," he said, immediately noticing the glazed look of her eyes. "What's wrong? And what are you doing here so late and alone? Where's Randall?"

The grilling summoned up the emotions she had promised herself to keep at bay once she stepped out of the cab. She wiped the water that began forming in her eyes.

Frowning at her, Linc checked his jacket feverishly for a hankie. Finding one, he blotted the tears rolling down her cheeks. "Jada, what's going on?"

"It hurts so much. I can't talk about it."

"Is it Randall? Did he do something to you?"

Biting her lip, she dropped her head.

Linc reared back, mystified. If he knew anything for certain in this world, Randall loved Jada. Randall loved her more than he had Selena. He loved her more than any other woman Linc had seen him involved with. "Let me take you somewhere where we can talk. Let's go to my yacht."

Linc grasped her hand and assisted her off of
the bar stool. She still looked shell-shocked by
something when he slipped his arm around her
shoulder and led her to the door. As they rode in si-
ence in his BMW, Linc glanced sideways at her
damp, stained face constantly. Craving to kiss
every tear away, he settled on sliding his hand in
hers, holding it firmly.

It relieved him that Jada showed no resistance.
She appeared to be so dazed with anguish that he
doubted she would resist anything tonight. His
thoughts were scrambling through his mind.
Thoughts that made him swallow repeatedly and
shift his weight in his seat to support the increasing mass of his loins.

"Careful now," he told her as she made the final
step up into the boat and nearly tripped. From the
back, he clutched her waist and guided her farther
in.

Inside the yacht, Jada stood looking like she
didn't know what to do.

"Have a seat," he offered and escorted her to
the chair nearby.

She plopped down and instantly laid her face in
her hands.

Linc kneeled in front of her. He lifted her hands
from her face, forcing her to look up at him. "How
did Randall hurt you?"

Jada's gaze scattered to various spots on the
floor, as if they showed pictures of the night's
events. "He is . . . he is with her again."

"Who?"

Her lips trembled. "Selena."

Linc released a sharp quick breath. He dropped

his head, shaking it, and then looked up at her again. "No. No, he wouldn't do that."

"I saw him. I mean he had to leave and I followed him. He went inside a shabby motel. I went inside and asked the clerk what room the man who just came in went to. He claimed he respected his patrons' privacy, so I threw a fifty-dollar bill at him and he lost that respect. The room belonged to Selena. Randall stayed in there for hours. He was still there when I left and went to the bar."

"Oh, man." Frowning, he sat next to her. "Randall is not nearly as smart as I thought he was."

"He is nowhere as trustworthy as I thought he was." She hopped up from the chair and paced. "I was so stupid! Why didn't I learn from my past with him and all the rest?"

"Jada, are you sure about this? Selena tried over and over to get back with Randall, but he acted like he'd rather die than take her back. Then she came back to me . . . and we hooked up again."

"Why did you do that? You know she really didn't want you."

"Why not? It's hard for a man to turn down a woman like that."

His words made her feel as if Selena possessed some magic that no other woman's charms could compare to. It saddened her that much more and she plopped back down on the couch.

Linc slipped his arms around her shoulders, simply holding her until she indicated that she wanted to lie down. He suggested some music to help her relax and put on Will Downing's latest CD. Listening to the lush music, he watched her sprawl sideways on the couch. Her eyes shut, but he knew she didn't sleep. He thought a cruise would help her further relax.

Moments later, they set sail on the ocean. Linc steered the yacht from the upper deck, and then joined her. She still lay sideways on his sofa, her eyes shut.

He flopped back against the wall gazing at the delicious sight. She had taken her sandals off and his eyes floated up her bare legs that were revealed from the skirt that had ridden up high on her thigh with her comfortable position. Her midriff top showed off her stomach and his scrutiny roamed up to her cleavage and soon to her face, to moist, slightly parted lips that he had longed to kiss since the first time he saw them.

Jada felt Linc's eyes on her and her own fluttered open. An urgent expression on his face, Linc strode straight toward her. Jada watched him kneel at her feet and, curious, raised her head to better view him. Her eyes closed and opened when creamy smooth lips glided like hot feathers across her toes. Jada tugged her feet back, but her quickening breaths encouraged him on. Gripping her ankles, Linc skimmed her calves with his lips.

"Stop it, Linc," she protested softly.

Linc's hands joined in the gratifying onslaught and his palms slid over the outside of her legs, thighs, before his fingertips moved to her lips and played with them. "I've wanted to put my tongue in your mouth and all over and *in* your beautiful body since the first time I saw you." He drew his face close to hers.

Jada turned her head, thwarting his lips from touching hers. "I can't do this."

"Yes, you can, baby," he whispered and attempted kissing her again.

Jada stood. "I better leave."

"No, Jada. You don't want to leave. You want to be with me. I can see it in your eyes. I can feel it." He walked behind her and grabbed her hand.

Coaxing her back against the wall, he raised her hands above her head. Ravenously he kissed along her neck until she lightly pushed him away.

"I'm not Selena, Linc. I'm not going to make love with you to get back at Randall. And if you were any kind of friend, you couldn't do that to him either."

"Randall still feels like a brother to me. There's no one else like him. But I'm a man, Jada, before I'm a friend. A flesh-and-blood man. And I'm also a man in love." He stared in her eyes.

She gazed back at him blankly. "I don't believe it when a man tells me he loves me anymore. It just doesn't have the same effect it used to. He can tell you he loves you one day like he'd die for you, and the next day he'll throw you away to die."

"I mean it. I've been in love with you for quite a while. You know, I was interested in you long before I even knew you knew Randall. I tried to put it aside and fight what I felt, but it just wouldn't go away. The last thing I wanted was a repeat of the situation with Selena. But this is different. I really, really love you, and I think you feel something for me, too."

"I do. I like you, Linc. As a friend. Yes, I'm flattered that you're attracted to me, and I find you attractive also. But there's a world of a difference between finding someone attractive and being attracted to them. Above all, even if Randall cheated on me, I'm not going to get back at him by being with you. It's so wrong, I wouldn't even enjoy it. Now, please bring this boat back to shore. I'd like to go home."

Chapter Twenty-four

After returning from Linc's boat, Jada entered her house feeling unlike herself. Her house didn't feel like her home. Nothing felt as if it should be. When her phone rang and she heard Randall speaking on her answering machine, she merely listened to him. He didn't seem like Randall anymore. But how could he be? The Randall Larimore she had fallen in love with was a fake. She trudged up her stairs and tried to go to sleep. By the time the sun rose the next morning, she had slept merely an hour.

When the phone rang again, she heard the voice of a nice, elderly tenant at the villas. They had become good friends. Mrs. Howard left a message for Jada, telling her how excited she was to attend the party for the hotel that evening. She promised to see her there. In all the hysteria of what had happened, Jada had nearly forgotten the party. The last place she wanted to be was partying with Randall.

Randall continued to call and leave messages

throughout the day. Finally she swiped up the phone.

"Hello," she answered in a monotone.

"I finally got you," he greeted her. "Baby, where were you? I called you last night and I've been calling all day."

Jada remained silent for several minutes and then answered, "I didn't feel well today and last night."

"Oh no, what's wrong? Want me to come over and fix you some soup or something? You do sound real nasal like you have a cold."

Jada sniffed back her tears. "I'm all right. You don't need to come over."

"Do you think you'll feel well enough to go to the party tonight?"

She cringed at being at the party with him. Yet her elderly friend would be there and would not know anyone. "I'll be there."

"What time should I pick you up?"

"I'll meet you there."

"No way. I'm walking in with my beautiful lady."

"And who is that?" she murmured.

"What? Baby, you sound so funny. You sure you're all right?"

"I'm okay."

"And I'm picking you up. I'm really excited about tonight. The press will be there. We had a lot of write-ups in the paper today, so I'm sure we're going to get party crashers. But anyway, I have a few things to wrap up. But I'll pick you up around 8:00 P.M. I love you and I want to thank you for sharing this dream with me. It's the first time I had a woman so strongly in my corner."

"Is that right?"

"Baby, are you sure you're all right?"

"I'm okay."

He made a kiss sound into the phone and added, "Bye."

Once she heard the click that concluded the call, Jada threw the phone across the room.

Later, when Randall picked Jada up, his eyes lit up at the red halter gown she wore. However, her facial expression didn't match. Her features held a mixture of sadness and anger. Over and over he asked her if anything was wrong.

She replied, "No" each time.

But she remained so silent during the car ride, Randall knew something was wrong. Sometime during the night, he planned to get her to open up. He felt a wall between them.

Once he arrived at the party, he was pulled in every direction away from her. Guests constantly engaged him in conversation. Other times, the press requested him to pose for pictures with Gus and Linc.

Amid it all, he noticed something that unnerved him. Ozzie and his crew attended the soiree despite Linc giving him his word that they wouldn't be allowed in. With their unwelcome appearance, Randall noticed them huddling into corners and later walking upstairs, where guests shouldn't have been. On one occasion, he followed them to a third-floor room. Outside the door, he listened.

"I've checked the others," Ozzie stated. "I've narrowed it down to this one."

"What are you talking about?" Randall inquired, emerging into the room.

Two of the men looked angered by his intrusion.

Ozzie snickered. "Man, what are you, a spy? You just don't like us, do you?"

"No," Randall answered flatly. "I don't trust you. And I want you out of these rooms. You have no business up here. Everything you need is downstairs."

"Man, we helped renovate this hotel," Ozzie went on. "Can't we take pride in our work?"

"I don't think that's what you were doing," Randall stated.

Ozzie laughed. "So what do you think we were doing?"

"I don't know," Randall answered. "But I know it's nothing good. Now if you don't mind, please go back downstairs."

After they left the room, Randall inspected it to see if everything remained in place. Everything looked fine. Still, he recalled that day Linc blabbed about the hidden money. Could they have been looking for it? At the same moment, he also thought about Selena describing the killers as Linc's friends.

Even though she swore they weren't Ozzie and his gang, he wondered. That's why he made Linc swear he wouldn't invite them to the grand-opening party tonight. He didn't want to be around them. Neither did he want to endanger Selena if she showed up.

After all, with no money she had to leave her motel. Where else could she turn to now, but Linc? All night he had watched the door, wondering if she would appear. All night he had also thought about explaining the circumstances with Selena to Jada.

Downstairs in the ballroom, Randall searched for Jada, but couldn't find her. He assumed she went to lie down in one of the rooms because she didn't feel well. Even when he asked the lady she had invited about Jada's whereabouts, she hadn't seen her either.

Eventually the crowd grew thin. Only a few waiters lingered in sight, along with Linc and Gus. Randall wanted to look for Jada, but Gus mentioned seeing her on the second floor. Randall felt relieved and planned to go to her as soon as he talked with Gus and Linc about Ozzie and his friends.

"They were up in one of the rooms and I knew they were up to something."

"Like what?" Linc asked with annoyance. "You've had it in for them since day one, Randall."

"Yes, you're being too harsh, son," Gus added. "They were probably just being nosy looking around the place. It is a pretty good looking establishment, if I do say so myself."

"No," Randall countered. "They were talking about something being in this specific room. I think they were up to something."

"Oh, man," Linc shot. "What is up with you? Why are you looking for trouble? You have everything, especially a *fine* woman who loves you."

Randall noted the way Linc spoke the word *fine* and the way he looked when he said it. "Yes, I do have everything."

"I hope you appreciate her," Linc said and walked off.

Randall had intended to tell Linc about Selena's predicament, but he disgusted him so much in that instant that he didn't want to talk to him anymore.

He had suspected that Linc wanted Jada, but he had no doubts in his mind now. It all made him feel protective of her. He sought her out upstairs where Gus said he saw her last. She wasn't there. He found her on the terrace. She stared into the darkness blankly.

"Having a good time?" he asked her.

Jada thought a moment before she answered, "No, I'm not, Randall."

"Why not?"

"I'm feeling homesick. I'm taking a leave of absence from work and going back to Jersey for a while. You should start looking for a replacement soon."

The news made Randall clutch his chest to temper his suddenly racing heart. He scowled at her. "What are you talking about?"

"I just told you. I'm taking a leave of absence and going home."

He shook his head. "No, you're not taking a leave of absence. You're leaving me, and I want to know why. What have I done? I thought we were happy. I thought everything was working out wonderfully. Where did this come from?"

"Where do you think?"

He threw his hands up. "I have no idea. I thought everything was perfect with us."

"Maybe everything is cool with you and *her*."

"Who? Another woman? What are you talking about?"

"I'm talking about Selena!" she snapped. "I followed you to her dingy motel yesterday."

"No, you have the wrong idea. I—"

She cut him off. "It's just like the old times. It's a pattern with you of going back to your exes." She began to sob. "But I won't let you break my heart this time."

"Oh, baby, you have it all wrong." He reached to hold her, but she pushed him back. "Jada, someone's trying to kill the woman. She asked for my help."

"That's a good one," she said with a laugh.

"It's the truth. She saw a murder. She—"

"I don't want to hear it." She started walking away.

He blocked her path, holding her arms. "No, you're going to hear this. I'm not letting you out of my life for some nonsense. This is a big misunderstanding."

Just then, Selena, wearing a gray satin gown, wandered onto the terrace.

Jada was shocked and gawked at Randall.

"Randall, the guards almost didn't let me in," Selena raved, hurrying toward them. "They said the festivities are over. I've been looking for you and Linc. I'm going to see if he will help me."

"Now that Selena is here," Randall said to Jada, "she can confirm what has been going on."

"So you're Jada," Selena said with an uneasy expression. "I've heard about you."

"I bet you have," Jada snapped, storming off the terrace. "I bet you two laughed a whole lot talking about me! You can have each other!"

Jada rushed away. Randall hurried behind her, only stopping when Linc pulled him aside.

"Gus is having some kinds of pain in his chest."

"Oh no," he said, watching Jada dash up the stairs. But knowing that Gus may have been having a heart attack, he couldn't follow her now. He raced to the couch Linc led him to.

Gus propped himself up until he sat up completely. "I'm all right."

"You sure?" Randall pressed.

"I've never felt better. I have gas. I know the difference between gas and a heart attack."

"Is everything all right?" Selena said, rushing toward them.

Linc's eyes widened seeing her. "What are you doing here?"

"She has a lot to tell you," Randall said, hurrying away. He headed up the stairs to catch up with Jada.

Jada located the room that had her shawl. She planned to get it and leave without Randall. However, the door was locked. Fortunately Randall had given her keys to every room in the inn. She searched her purse for this room's key and unlocked the door.

As soon as she pushed it open, Jada wished she never had a key to this room. Ozzie and his two friends had busted open a safe. Money lay all over the floor. Jada made a motion to flee.

Ozzie grabbed her, covering her mouth. One of his friends locked the door.

Downstairs Linc and Selena secluded themselves to talk since they knew Gus was fine.

"How have you been?" he asked her.

"All right," she said, and then started to cry.

"What's the matter?"

"They're trying to kill me."

Linc cocked his head to hear her better. He

knew what he heard, but it had to be his imagination playing tricks. "You couldn't have said that someone is trying to kill you?"

"Ozzie and his friends."

"What?" he shouted.

"I saw them kill that politician that they found murdered here on the island. They did it. I was on the docks, coming to see you, and I saw them beat him, shoot him, and throw him in the water."

Linc had a flash of Ozzie offering to throw Randall in the river after Randall busted his lip. He had assumed Ozzie kidded him. "Ozzie was here tonight."

"Oh my God," she cried. "Is he gone?"

"He should be. I think everyone has left. I saw the waiters just leave, so the only ones here should be Randall, Jada, and Gus, and you and me. But don't worry. We'll take care of this. I won't let him or anyone hurt you."

Upstairs Randall had searched every room for Jada except one in which the door seemed to be jammed with something. When he heard mumbling in the room, he knew no one should have been in there. Something was wrong.

He tried to knock the door down with his body force. When that didn't work, he went to a tool closet and found a hammer. Over and over he tried to break the lock with it.

Hearing the commotion downstairs, Gus, Linc, and Selena hurried upstairs. They saw Randall trying to break open the door.

"I think Jada is in there and I sense something is wrong," he told them. "I heard sounds."

Linc rushed to the tool closet and retrieved another hammer, then back to Randall's side to assist him. "I hope Ozzie isn't in there with her. Selena just told me he murdered someone and has been after her."

Randall looked over at Selena. "I thought you said it wasn't him."

"I was scared, Randall."

"I'll go call the police," Gus said, rushing down the stairs.

Randall and Linc proceeded hitting the door with the hammers. When they finally managed to break the lock, they kicked the door open. They found Ozzie, his two companions, and Jada looking terrified within Ozzie's grasp. Money scattered over the floor.

Randall went for Ozzie, punching him, while Linc charged at one of the others. Selena tried to sneak out, but the unoccupied man grabbed her and pulled out a gun.

"We've been looking for you, little lady."

Ozzie managed to grab the gun from him and Randall backed off of him. He took turns aiming the barrel at everyone. "No one is getting out of here the way they came in, but me and my two friends."

"I told you not to trust them," Randall told Linc. At the same time, he divided his scrutiny between the gun and Jada. Freed from Ozzie's clutches, she eased to the door.

"Ozzie, what are you doing, man?" Linc asked.

"I'm getting money. What do you think?" Then he gazed at Selena. "And I've been looking so long for you, hot stuff." He aimed the gun at her head.

Tears streamed down Selena's cheeks.

"Man, don't kill anyone else," Linc pleaded. "You're in enough trouble."

"I'm in no trouble at all. She's not going to live to tell anyone what she saw. And none of you will live to tell anything either."

Randall eyed Jada. She continued making her way to the door.

Ozzie came closer to Selena.

Linc jumped forward to knock the gun away, but one of the other guys grabbed him, flinging him aside.

But no sooner had Jada sneaked her way to the door entrance than Ozzie came toward her. "You're not going anywhere. In fact, I might do you right here in front of your man."

Randall leaped on him and tried to wrestle the gun from his hands. Linc jumped on one of the others. Seeing the third man distracted, Jada fled out of the room. Selena sped out behind her. But the unoccupied member of Ozzie's crew refused to let them get away. He pulled a knife from his jacket and dashed out of the room hot on their trail.

The women saw Gus as they fled downstairs and out of the hotel. He ran out with them until exhaustion slowed him and the man caught up with him. The thug slung his knife at Gus, slicing his arm. Gus rolled on the ground in pain. He watched the brute proceed to chase Jada and Selena.

A boat sat at the edge of the shoreline. Jada and Selena hopped into it and began rowing as fast as they could.

Upstairs in the room, the gun had gone off several times. Randall and Ozzie wrestled until Ozzie managed to aim the barrel at Randall's temple. Linc, seeing what was about to happen, laid a brutal blow against his adversary, knocking him out. Then he had to rescue Randall. He leaped up toward Ozzie's hand, knocking the gun on the floor and away from Randall's head.

Breathless, Randall eyed him. "Thank you."

"Anytime," Linc replied.

Knowing they had no time to lose, Randall and Linc tied the men up and rushed outside. They saw Gus bleeding, but felt relief when he said he would be okay. He pointed toward the ocean. They saw the boat with Jada and Selena rowing feverishly. The rogue swam toward them and turned over the boat.

Linc and Randall dived in the water. Linc caught up to the man and choked him until he sank. At that same instant, Randall headed toward Jada and Selena. Neither could swim and both were drowning.

"Help me!" Selena cried. "Help me, Randall!"

"I'm drowning!" Jada hollered.

Randall reached an equal distance among both women. Yet he had no indecision about whom to rescue first. He raced to Jada and brought her safely to shore. Afterward he saved Selena.

Moments later, as the two women sat receiving medical attention, Selena laid her hand on Jada's. "Randall loves you so much." She looked down sadly. "He saved you first. But that wasn't a surprise to me. He told me how much he loved you when he came to see me." She went on to talk about the murder she had witnessed and how she had shared that horror with Randall.

Guilt overwhelmed Jada when Randall had a

moment alone with her. "I love you, Jada," he
said. "Nothing was going on with Selena and me

"I know, baby," she said, hugging him. "I love
you, too. And thank you for saving my life."

Later, in the wee hours of the morning, Randall
carried Jada up the stairs of his mansion and into
his bedroom's shower. On the way home she had
told him over and over that she wanted to shower.
She felt clammy, dirty, and itchy.

Soon he let her down at the bathroom door
while he went about things in the bedroom. Jada
entered the peach-colored bathroom, turned on
the knobs for the shower, and shed her clothes.
Soon the water poured over her naked form.
Thanking God for sparing Randall's life, hers, and
everyone else's that had been in danger, she closed
her eyes.

The cool air from the shower curtain being
pushed aside caused her eyes to flutter open. Naked
Randall stood staring at her. His body was so rigid
and ready for her, she drew in a breath. Randall
came toward her and slid his hands over her wet
bare form. Kisses sprinkled all over her body, and
he started their magic all over again at her feet.

Randall suckled her toes while she lowered her
hands, playing in his hair. His pleasure crusade crept
upward with him kissing her ankles and calves ever
so tenderly. Jada thought the aching need welling
up in her would burst. Randall brought her to a
new level of excitement when he kissed her inner
thighs and spread them apart with his face, as he
sought the honey between them. Sensation after
sensation of ecstasy washed over her, drenching
her with her own love juices.

When Randall knew she was ready for his full loving, he sheathed his manhood. Then backing her against the wall, he raised her hands above her head, giving his tongue free exploration of her breasts and nipples. Jada cried out as the ache of pleasure knotted in her core, driving her out of her mind. And then when she could barely take anymore, he forced her legs apart. He guided his love into her.

Pumping her hard while he kissed her, Jada felt joy wash over her that drove her near senseless. Every time Randall filled her with love, it drenched her with addictive pleasure that made her beg for more.

So hot that he couldn't stand it, Randall was determined to give her even more rapture. He swung Jada around, forcing the front of her against the wall. From the back, he slid his erection over her backside with titillating movements that drove him insane. He became turned on even more, hearing her begging and moaning for him to place his love inside her once again.

About to burst from his growing and growing excitement, he soon obliged her. He filled her love with himself and nearly died with ecstasy as they swayed to a blissfully magical rhythm. When the tide became too much, they shook and the orgasmic satisfaction nearly drained them.

A short time later, they lay on their bed, their bodies slick from lovemaking and water. Randall began to kiss all over her all over again. He could barely speak, she thrilled him so. Still he managed to whisper, "Will you marry me, Jada? I love you so much."

Jada froze with the shock of the beautiful words. "Yes," she said, sobbing into his mouth as he kissed her deeply.

They decided to take a trip to see their families and spread the good news about their engagement. Randall also wanted to see his brother Jackson's baby. The infant had been born premature, but was thriving just fine. At a Larimore family gathering, after everyone had stuffed their bellies with grand-style soul food, Jackson, Randall's near twin, handed his little son, Brandell, to Randall.

"His name kind of sounds like yours," Jackson said, watching his brother holding the baby as if it would break.

"Oh, this child is so good looking, he must take after his uncle, too."

Everyone laughed.

Jada smiled, imagining Randall holding their child.

Randall's five-year-old niece, Hannah, also observed her uncle holding the baby so carefully and stood next to him, patting his knee. "Don't worry, Uncle Randy, he won't break. And you better learn how to hold him right because Mama told Grandmama you're going to have one of these soon."

Everyone in the family started laughing.

Later, Kelly escorted Jada to her old room where they could talk.

Jada hugged her. "Oh, thank you, Kelly. You were certainly a sneak, but a good sneak. It led to something good."

Kelly's hazel eyes sparkled. "Girl, I knew you and my brother were made for each other."

"He's so wonderful, Kelly. Sometimes I feel unworthy."

"Girl, please. Wait until Randall starts getting on your nerves. You're going to be calling me telling me off."

"Never," Jada swore and they laughed and talked the afternoon away.

After Jada spent a great deal of time with Kelly, Hannah came and got Jada. She claimed that Randall's parents, Claire and Johnny, wanted to see her in the study.

Jada was nervous as she walked into the room and beheld two somber faces.

"Don't worry, dear," Claire said, her hazel eyes watering. "We just wanted to tell you thank you for making Randall so happy. My boy is happier than I have ever seen him."

"And I echo that sentiment," Johnny added. He then took Jada's hand and patted it. "He told us that you were the young lady he fell in love with long ago. We are so sorry for guiding him in another direction back then."

"But we didn't know any better back then," Claire added. "We thought it was more honorable to have him stick by the young lady because she was in an accident and also because of their baby. I'm sure you know the story."

"I understand," Jada said and hugged each of them. "God had a plan for Randall and me to be in each other's lives, and nothing could stop that. And I know that you two thought you were doing the right thing. I'm grateful to have such caring in-laws-to-be. I know you are who Randall gets his wonderful values from and I will never feel alone again."

"Welcome to the family, dear," Claire said. "We'r so happy to have you in our circle of love."

"Welcome, my daughter," Johnny added.

The next day Randall showed Jada his home in Lakeside. She loved it, but thought the decorating needed a woman's touch. He told her to decorate it in any manner she pleased. He also asked her i she preferred living there to St. Thomas. She told him that they could live in both places, especially since it was near his family. However, she told him that the tropical paradise would always hold a spe cial place in her heart. It was the place where the fell in love.

Days later, they arrived in New Jersey and visited her family. Her mother and grandmother fixed Randall and Jada a special soul food dinner com plete with all the works—fried chicken, potato salad, and collard greens.

Katherine's children were also ecstatic that they could visit their aunt's new house in St. Thomas. A for Randall, they immediately adored him as he told them about his travels around the world, pur chasing property, and that he would take them along.

When Jada found herself alone with her sister Katherine, she was surprised at how much happier Katherine seemed.

"Why are you glowing, big sis?" she asked her.

Katherine's round face flushed. "I met some one. He's so nice, Jada."

Jada was taken aback. "You mean a man?"

Katherine smiled. "He works in the building where I receive therapy. He's a dentist, a very nice man. We've gone out on a few dates, although I haven't told Mama and Grandmama. He wants to meet my kids, too."

"Are you going to let him?"

Katherine nodded, shaking a head of black, shiny curls. "I think so. I'm so tired of being sad, and bored. I want to live again, little sis. And he makes me feel like I'm living. He makes me feel alive again. It's been so long since I felt that way. It feels like I'm breathing air again instead of smothering. You know what I mean?"

Jada thought of herself. "Oh yes, I know what you mean."

"You seem like you're feeling the same way. I can see Randall makes you happy. And I can feel the love between you two. It's real, real strong. When I had my breakdown I became sensitive to things like that. Your love is so strong, Jay. Hold on to it and enjoy your happiness. He seems like a real good man."

Downstairs, Randall stirred around in the kitchen with Jada's mother and grandmother, clearing the dishes off the table. The two women truly enjoyed him as he talked about how delicious the food was and the nice time he had with them. As Grandmama Cicley prepared to wash the dishes, Randall grabbed her hand, along with Jada's mother, Mary.

"I want to thank you two so much," he told them.

Grandmama Cicley patted his hand. "Son, having you in our home has been our pleasure."

"Yes, it has," Mary agreed.

"And I want you both to know something. I love Jada."

"I can see that," Mary said with a smile.

"And I will never ever do anything to hurt her. If we have a disagreement, we will try and work it out. I know how hurt she has been, and I will never do that to her. My entire life is going to be devoted to making her happy. That makes me happy when I know she is. So don't you worry about her. She is truly loved."

Jada called Randall upstairs, leaving the two women alone.

Grandmama Cicley wore a warm smile. "I have a good feeling about that young man. And my first feeling is always correct. When Jada brought her first husband home, I had a bad feeling. I didn't feel right when she brought Michael home either. It's just instinct. But not this young man. He's a good man. Not because he's rich either. He's just a good man from the heart. I can feel it."

Mary nodded her agreement. "I feel it, too, Mama. Our baby has finally found the love of a lifetime—the love that comes once in a lifetime if you're lucky."

Cicley looked up to the ceiling. "The Lord is sure enough watching over their souls."

Chapter Twenty-five

Ocean waves leaped up and crashed back down against the island shore. They were just another attraction for the three hundred guests that mingled nearby on Randall's estate. He had flown in much of his family for the wedding, including aunts, uncles, cousins, and many friends. Much of Jada's family and friends also attended the nuptials.

Multicolored roses decorated the white patio tables and chairs that scattered about the lawn. Waiters served hors d'oeuvres while a band played an instrumental of "Always and Forever." Hunter, Jackson, Tyler, and Dustin Larimore, Randall's brothers and near twins, stood aside checking out each other's white tuxedos before the wedding started.

"I can't *believe* Randall is getting married," Hunter said with an urgency in his voice. "What's happening to all the players? Our club is getting real small."

Smiling, Jackson laid his hand on his brother's

shoulders. "My man, you were the only player in this family."

Dustin and Tyler slapped hands.

"And how ya'll handsome boys doing?" their aunt Essie May said, stepping among the group of four. You four are looking mighty fine today."

"You look fabulous, too," Dustin complimented her and saw the others nod their agreement.

"Thank you," she gushed, patting her short curls. "This is going to be a fabulous ceremony. Look at this place. I'm so proud of Randall. I'm proud of all you boys. You're all doing so well."

"Thank you," Jackson said.

Hunter, Dustin, and Tyler agreed in unison.

"You know, I had a vision," she went on.

The brothers eyed each other nervously. Aunt Essie May was famous in the family for being psychic. If she dreamed about you, you had better expect luck or look out for falling concrete.

"I dreamed about you getting married, Jackson. Don't you remember I told you that a year before you got married?"

Jackson thought for a moment. His face brightened at the memory. "You sure did."

"And I had a vision about Randall getting married, too. I told him about it at your wedding, Jackson. He didn't believe me, but look at us at his wedding today."

"Wow," Tyler remarked.

"So what is the vision you were just going to tell us about?" Dustin asked. "Is it . . . is it about me?" he asked cautiously.

Aunt Essie May looked straight at Hunter. "Sorry, son. Your big brother here is the one I've seen in my last visions."

"Me?" Hunter said as if the news were poisonous.

"I sure did. You're the next one to get married. I've seen it clear as day."

Someone calling Aunt Essie May took her away and among a crowd.

Hunter shook his head. "No way in the world I'm the next to get married. I'm never giving up my player card."

Jackson looked at him laughing. "Watch out. She's been right so far."

"What's wrong with settling down?" Dustin teased.

Hunter frowned at him. "I don't see you tying yourself to the old ball and chain."

"He hasn't found the right one yet," Tyler added. "Just like I haven't, but I'm open."

"Well, I'm not! I'm never, ever getting married. And if I see Aunt Essie May again, I'm staying away from her. Some have said she's a bit touched, and I believe that if she thinks I'm getting married. Not in this lifetime."

"We'll see," Jackson said, watching his brother float away toward two attractive women. "We will see." He smiled.

In a bedroom in the mansion, Randall's dad, Johnny, helped his son with his tie.

"I'm so proud of you. And I'm so glad that you picked a woman who makes you so happy. I see it all over you, son—the happiness."

Randall smiled and hugged his dad. When they released, Linc stood in the doorway.

Johnny, knowing Linc's and his son's history, wasn't sure if he should leave the two alone. "You okay with this, son?"

"Linc and I are cool, Dad." He patted him on the shoulder.

Johnny left the room.

Linc stepped toward Randall. "Congratulations. And thank you for giving me the chance to talk to you."

"How could I not?" Randall said. "A gun cocked at my head and you saved me."

"Because you're my friend, Randall. Regardless of what happened with Selena and me, you're my friend. And I wish you lots of happiness. You and Jada are very lucky that you've found each other. I hope to have that type of relationship one day."

Randall looked him deep in the eyes. "You do the right thing and anything can happen."

"I am trying to do the right thing. I sent Selena home and gave her some money to get settled back in Lakeside. But if you're wondering if we're together again, we're not. She always loved you, Randall. Just like Jada loves you. You're a very lucky man."

"Are you staying for the ceremony?"

"No, but I wish you the best. Good luck." Linc extended his hand to Randall.

Randall shook it and noted a hint of somberness from Linc. When he left, Randall acknowledged what it was. Linc didn't want to stay for the wedding because he didn't want to see him marry Jada. He was in love with her and he wanted her. But Randall guessed that life had taught his old friend a lesson: sometimes you couldn't have everything you wanted.

Sometimes what you wanted could make you lose something valuable—like friendship. Sometimes you just had to do what was right. He knew Linc couldn't stop feeling for Jada what he did, no more than he could. Then again, no one could help feeling something so deeply in their heart. They could only help what they did about it.

Moments later, Jada stood at the aisle with one arm laced in her mother's. The other arm held her grandmother. She knew their escorting her down the aisle went against tradition. But, these were the two that had raised and loved her during her life. Still she was grateful to her father, who sat in the front row.

As she walked, her gaze was riveted to her handsome husband-to-be. Randall took her breath away in his white tuxedo and with his loving gaze straight into her eyes. Jada's heart beat so fast as she looked at him that she forced her attention elsewhere. Otherwise, she wouldn't make it down the aisle without crying.

Her suntanned skin glowed against the white, chiffon, off-the-shoulder gown with a semicathedral train. A three-tiered pearl choker strikingly accentuated the dress. Her upswept hairstyle, which allowed a few tendrils to skim her shoulders, complemented her soft pink makeup.

Walking and trying not to look at her gorgeous man and cry, Jada glanced to each side of the aisle. She smiled at the guests for sharing this amazing occasion with her. She spotted Ms. Emma's proud face among the guests and winked at her. She could never forget what she once told her: "There's something that I've heard all my life. First heard grown folks saying it when I was barely able to talk. Didn't know what it meant then, but God knows I know now. And that is if someone really, really loves you, and you're meant to be together, somehow or some way, they will come into your life again. It may not happen when you want. It may not happen the way you want. It may not happen until years and years and years from now, but if it's meant to be, you will be part of each other's lives again in this lifetime."

At last, Jada stood beside Randall living the reality of those words. Randall and she had found their way back into each other's lives because it was God's divine plan. Out of all the men in the world, He had created this man for her to love. Out of all the women in the world, He had created her to love this man. They felt for each other what they felt for no one else. They felt for each other what they could only feel with each other.

"Family and friends of Jada and Randall," the Reverend Ashton Hardaway said, pushing his glasses up by the middle. "Thank you for coming to share this wonderful occasion as they become husband and wife. The bride and groom have thoughts that they would like to share with each other before they are blessed with the traditional vows." He nodded toward Jada.

Feeling the pressure of tears fighting to fall from her eyes, Jada turned to face Randall. "Randall, I want to thank God for bringing you into my life. All of my life, I've dreamed of that special kind of love, where someone would love me with all his heart and soul. I dreamed of being the person that some man loved like he had never loved anyone else. Over and over I thought I'd found that type of love. But it always turned out to be wrong. I was always hurt. I had decided that love just wasn't meant for me. And I tried to go on and live without it. But you . . . you changed all that. You welcomed me into your life and into your heart. You are a man of integrity and kindness, and a man so filled with love, I am now touched with it. You make me feel so precious, so beautiful, and so loved. Every day with you I feel like magic is happening to me. I want to thank you for loving me and showing me that I can love again. I want to thank you for coming into my life and saving me with your love. Again, I thank God for your precious love and I will treasure it for the rest of my life." With her finger, she dabbed at the corner of her eye, where a tear had formed. "I love you so much, Randall."

Randall stared at Jada for several seconds before holding her face gently within his hands. "Jada, I thank God for you, too. I wake up every day thanking Him for bringing you into my life. I used to get up and go to work every day and come home with nothing to look forward to. I was broken because love hadn't been kind to me either. But when you came into my life, it was like the sun shined on me even at night. Now I get up every day thinking of you and feeling so happy that I have a woman that I love so much and who loves me in return. I go about my work with a new feeling because always in the back of my mind I know that work is not all I have. I have you. I think about you when I work, when I drive, when I do everything and anything. I always feel this strong, passionate love for you no

matter what I'm doing or where I go. I never knew
it was possible to feel so much love for someone
and I want to cherish you and show you how much
I love you every day of my life. I have never, ever
felt for any woman what I feel for you. You are
beautiful. You are intelligent. You are loving. You
are caring. You are funny. You're unselfish. And
you have something so special about you that af-
fects me so deeply. It's something that I can't even
describe. I want to do everything and anything to
please you and make you happy. I have a new purpose to my life. In everything I do to be successful
in this life, I know I will be doing it for the both of
us. Everyone here is my witness that I will honor
you and treat you as a queen, which you are, and
that you should be treated as. You are my life. I will
be there to hold you, comfort you, and take care of
you in sickness and in health. And I love you, Jada.
I love you so much and I know there is only one
woman on this earth for me. And God sent her to
me. Again, I thank Him for sending me you, Jada.
I love you so much. So very, very much."

Randall kissed Jada passionately. The guests
smiled and even murmured because he would not
let her go.

The reception prolonged the bliss on the Larimore estate. One of St. Thomas's most prominent
restaurants, the Paramour, served guests a variety
of meals from its extensive list of dishes. A fountain
poured an assortment of tropical drinks, along
with spirits. A band serenaded everyone with soul-
stirring oldies-but-goodies music as well as from

oday's soul and jazz artists. Everyone was on the dance floor, even Jada's grandma Cicley.

During the band's breaks, guests were treated to the DJ's collection of ballads by crooners Luther Vandross, Phil Perry, Will Downing, Rachelle Farrelle, Deborah Cox, Tamia, Alicia Keyes, Prince, Gerald Levert, Gladys Knight, and Aretha Franklin. The song selection reflected Jada and Randall's love for old school music. A poetry reading and an African dance number rounded out the entertainment at the wedding. Toasts were scattered throughout the reception festivities, most were funny. Others were very touching, then came the time for Randall's toast.

He stood at the center of the grounds holding up a glass of champagne, while two waiters wheeled a table to him. Neither Jada nor anyone else knew what he was up to.

"I wanted to give my beautiful bride something that she always wanted."

"That's you!" Kelly shouted, making everyone laugh.

"I have something else that she wanted," he said, gazing into Jada's eyes. Suddenly he lifted a cloth, which covered an item on the table the waiter had wheeled over. It was a model of a bookstore. It had three floors.

Jada's hand's flew up to her mouth. "Oh my God."

"This is a model of your bookstore, baby. It has three floors. The top floor will be for signings, readings, and other entertainment if you so desire. The second floor will be for patrons who have browsed and just want to sit down and read. So it will look almost like a library. A café will be on the floor, too. And the first floor will contain the shelve and shelves of books. I've started construction o it downtown. This is your dream."

Tearful, Jada embraced him and then kissed hir deeply. "Thank you, baby. Thank you so much You are my dream."

Everyone clapped. When they settled down, Rar dall pulled out a pair of keys and looked at Jada family. "Ms. Gracen, Grandma Cicley, Katherine Keisha, Diane, Deandre, and Shyquain, I had mansion that was just sitting there. Built it fo someone, but it didn't work out. So the keys to thi mansion, are now yours. This way you can be b your beloved Jada any time you want."

Everyone in the family, including Jada, rushee to him, hugging him for his generosity.

In Randall's master bedroom, Jada woke up afte a long, restful sleep and looked over at Randall who slept holding her. They had made sizzling-ho love for hours, exhausting themselves, and gone off fast asleep.

Randall stretched about until he noticed he looking at him. "Hello, Mrs. Larimore."

Jada smiled. "Hello, Mr. Larimore."

He brushed her hair. "Am I dreaming?"

"Then I'm dreaming with you."

"You sure you don't want to go on a honey moon?"

"Oh, Randall, I feel like I'm on a honeymoor every moment that I'm with you. As long as w keep our love as strong and beautiful as it is at thi moment, we're going to feel happier than we eve

magined. I can't be any happier than I am at this
moment."

"Neither can I, baby. And I will love you for-
ver." He eased his lips toward hers.

She kissed him deep, passionately, and with all
he love that she held within her. For she knew, this
vas truly the love of a lifetime.

Dear Reader:

I am so grateful that you allowed me to entertain you with Jada and Randall's romance. I wanted you to experience their passionate love and be swept away into a world that reminds you what is worth cherishing in this life. I also wanted to make you feel that all dreams are possible—because I truly believe they are.

Thank you for the emails, letters, and cards. Each one I receive is a gift that I treasure. Many wrote me about *If Loving You Is Wrong* and wanted Randall to have his own story. I hope his story entertained you, uplifted you, and made you feel hopeful about love and relationships.

I love receiving mail. Please feel free to write me at *Lourebus@aol.com*, or P.O. Box 020648, Brooklyn, New York 11203-0648. And I'd love for you to visit me on the web at LoureBussey.com. May God bless you all with love, happiness, and success.

                                        Until next time,
                                        Louré Bussey

About the Author

Louré Bussey is the author of the novels *Nightfall, Most Of All, Twist Of Fate, Love So True, A Taste Of Love, Images Of Ecstasy Dangerous Passions, Just The Thought Of You,* and *If Loving You Is Wrong.* Her books have appeared on Ingram and Amazon's bestseller lists. She is also a singer/songwriter/record producer and business owner.

More Arabesque Romances by
Donna Hill

__TEMPTATION	0-7860-0070-8	$4.99US/$5.99CAN
__A PRIVATE AFFAIR	1-58314-158-8	$5.99US/$7.99CAN
__CHARADE	0-7860-0545-9	$4.99US/$6.50CAN
__INTIMATE BETRAYAL	0-7860-0396-0	$4.99US/$6.50CAN
__PIECES OF DREAMS	1-58314-183-9	$5.99US/$7.99CAN
__CHANCES ARE	1-58314-197-9	$5.99US/$7.99CAN
__A SCANDALOUS AFFAIR	1-58314-118-9	$5.99US/$7.99CAN
__SCANDALOUS	1-58314-248-7	$5.99US/$7.99CAN
__THROUGH THE FIRE	1-58314-130-8	$5.99US/$7.99CAN

Available Wherever Books Are Sold!

Check out our website at www.BET.com.

BOOK YOUR PLACE ON OUR WEBSITE
AND MAKE THE ARABESQUE
ROMANCE CONNECTION!

We've created a customized website just for our very special Arabesque readers, where you can get the inside scoop on everything that's going on with Arabesque romance novels.

When you come online, you'll have the exciting opportunity to:

- View covers of upcoming books

- Learn about our future publishing schedule (listed by publication month and author)

- Find out when your favorite authors will be visiting a city near you

- Search for and order backlist books

- Check out author bios and background information

- Send e-mail to your favorite authors

- Join us in weekly chats with authors, readers and other guests

- Get writing guidelines

- AND MUCH MORE!

Visit our website at
http://www.arabesquebooks.com